Making the Squad

Written by Tasha Fuller

Illustrated by Racheal Scotland

Your Go2 Girls

MW00930658

i

Making the Squad is Published by Your Go2 Girls

Woodbridge, VA

www.TashasBooks.com

Copyright © 2017 Tasha Fuller

All rights reserved. No part of this book may be used or reproduced in any manner whatsoever in whole or in part, or stored in a retrieval system, or transmitted in any form or by any means, electronic, mechanical, photocopy, recording or otherwise without the written permission, of the publisher, except in the case of brief quotations embodied in critical articles and reviews.

Library of Congress Control Number: 2019912698

ISBN: 978-0-9860656-2-0

DEDICATION

To my children: Aukema, Freddie, Amira and Ellis for always being a source of endless inspiration. To my husband Freddie for his support. To my mother Hattie for being the ultimate example of hard work, determination and courage. To my dad Tony for being my #1 Sales Agent. To all friends, family members and fans who continue to support and encourage me to write.

To my Lord and Savior Jesus Christ who makes all things possible.

CONTENTS

ACKNOWLEDGEMENTS

Racheal Scotland an amazing Illustrator who is more than patient with my process and brings my stories to life with her amazing talents.

Cheerleader Extraordinaire and Best Neighbor Ever, Deidra Knight

Carol Patterson, Editor

Freddie C. Fuller II, Editor

Jahleen Wright, Editor

Elementary School

CHAPTER 1

I have been cheering since I was seven years old and I remember it like it was yesterday. I started when my best friend Taylor's twin brother, Tyler, was playing tackle football on a little league team. Taylor was on the team's cheerleading squad. Her mom, Ms. Dee, was the cheerleading coach and her dad, Mr. Omar, was one of the football coaches.

My twin brother, Freddie, and I were playing soccer at the time, but when I found out

Taylor was cheering. I begged my mom to let me cheer too.

"No, you're already playing soccer," Mom protested.

"But, Mommy! Mommy! I really want to be a cheerleader. Can't I do both?" I pleaded.

"No, it's just too much. I am sure there is going to be some type of conflict between soccer, cheerleading practices, and games. Your Daddy and I are already trying to manage you and your brothers' practices, games, and after school activities. Not to mention all your older sister, Aukema's activities," she reminded me.

"But Mommy, Ms. Dee said I can ride with her to practices, and it's okay for me to come after my soccer games if there was a conflict," I negotiated.

"Amira, why do you want to keep adding things to our already busy schedule?" Mommy countered.

"Please, please, please Mommy! I really want to be a cheerleader, and I can just quit soccer," I tried to bargain, thinking I could lighten my parents load by only doing one sport.

"Um, no ma'am! We are not quitters. Your team is depending on you and you already made the commitment. Might I remind you, you are the one who said you wanted to play soccer again and I am sure the league won't refund our registration fee at this point," she answered.

I could tell by her tone she was disgusted by my suggestion because she doesn't believe in quitting. She had been coaching basketball since before I was born, and she never lets her players quit. I have been to countless practices where her players were throwing up, crying or completely exhausted, but they always had to finish.

"Quitters never win, and winners never quit," is one of her many sayings. *I guess that's why she has won so many championships and her former players are always calling and coming around even after they've graduated.* She never quit on them, and she certainly wouldn't let them quit on themselves.

"Let me discuss it with your Dad, and I will talk to Ms. Dee," Mommy said.

"Great!" I said to myself. At least it's no longer a definite *"No,"* There's a possibility of a "Yes," Knowing Daddy, I am sure he would go along with whatever Mom decided, so it was up to Ms. Dee to convince her. The next day at the bus stop I knew I had to talk to Taylor.

"What did she say?" Taylor asked with anticipation.

"She said she would think about it,"

"Well what does that mean and how long will that take?"

"I don't know. She said that she would discuss it with my Dad and talk to your Mom,"

"Well when will you know?" she asked again.

"I don't know, but what I do know, if I keep asking her before she has a chance to think about it, she is definitely going to say no," I warned.

"Oh," Taylor responded. I could tell she was a little disappointed that it wasn't going to be an easy *yes*.

"Don't worry Taylor. We just have to make sure we talk to your mom after school, so she can convince my mom to say yes," I reassured her.

"Great! That sounds like a plan!" Taylor agreed.

Making The Squad

All day during school we talked about what we could say to Ms. Dee to help her convince my Mommy to allow me to cheer. We strategized at lunch, during recess, and on the bus ride home. We even continued our strategy session after we'd finished our homework and were outside playing. As soon as Ms. Dee pulled into the driveway, we rushed over to plead our case.

Being next door neighbors worked to our advantage when we wanted to do something or wanted to get something done. What are the odds of two sets of boy and girl twins who are the same age, in the same grade, living right next door to each other? Taylor and I were even in the same class for two years straight. People used to think Taylor and I were twins and Freddie and Tyler were twins. But my Mommy disagrees. She says *no one says that, except me ...! But I digress*.

"Mommy, Mommy, Mommy!" Taylor shouted to gain her mother's full attention.

"Ms. Dee, I talked to my mom about cheerleading, and she said that she wants to talk to you," I informed her.

"Mommy, Ms. Tasha says it's too much for Amira to do two sports with everything else they have going on. Will you please tell her that it's okay for Amira to join the team, and she can just ride with us?" Taylor pleaded.

"Chile, I can't tell another mother what to do with her child," Ms. Dee responded.

"But Mommy," Taylor pleaded again.

"Ms. Dee, I really want to be on the cheerleading squad. Can you please talk to my Mommy?" I chimed in, begging her too.

"Bye girls," Ms. Dee said as she dismissed us and walked into the house.

Well that certainly didn't go as planned. We didn't even stick to the script we had come up with at school. I don't know if our conversation with Ms. Dee helped or hurt my chances of being on the team, but we tried.

It was getting dark and the street lights were coming on, so I knew it was time for me to go in the house to eat dinner and get ready for bed. When I came in the house my mom didn't mention anything about cheerleading, not even during dinner. I took my shower and got dressed for bed. As we prepared to say our night time prayers, I wanted to ask my Mommy if she had decided about cheer, but I knew better than to bring it up. My Mommy hates to be harassed when she says she is going to think about something. If you ask her again before she's ready to answer, it's almost always a definite, *No.*

The suspense was driving me crazy, but I knew I had to be patient and wait. I learned that by watching my older sister Aukema get denied countless times because she wasn't patient enough to wait for Mommy to give her an answer. "Stop harassing me," I recall her saying. So, I waited and kept my mouth shut and just as we were finishing our night time prayers, I heard the doorbell. "Lord, I hope that's Ms. Dee," I prayed quietly.

My mom kissed us all good night and went downstairs to answer the door. It was Ms. Dee.

"Thank you, Jesus," I quietly said to myself. They exchanged "*Hey Neighbor,*" and hugs, and sat in the front room to talk, and when I say talk, that's exactly what they did. They must have talked for at least an hour before they even mentioned cheerleading. I know because I was in the upstairs landing listening to the whole conversation.

"So, what's up with cheerleading?" my mom asked.

"Girl, you know I got you," Ms. Dee responded.

"Well, I guess she can do it. Just send me the details," my mom reluctantly agreed.

Are you kidding me! That's it. Their whole conversation about cheerleading was less than a minute. Taylor and I spent all day trying to figure out ways to convince my mom to let me cheer, and all Ms. Dee says is *"I got you,"* for my mom to consent? What in the world?

They talked a little more, before Mommy walked Ms. Dee to the door. They hugged good bye, and Mommy watched her as she walked back home. When Mommy locked the door and headed up the stairs, I quickly made my way to my room, so my mom wouldn't notice that I was being nosy and being up an hour past my bedtime. I could hear her as she reached the top of the stairs, so I pretended to be asleep.

"Don't act like you're sleeping. I heard you running to your room. I guess you already know. I am going to let you cheer," she said.

I leaped from my bed squealing with excitement. I hugged her as tight as I possibly could. "Thank you! Thank you, Mommy, thank you!" I repeated as I hugged and kissed her. "I can't wait to tell Taylor!"

CHAPTER 2

Normally Taylor and Tyler came to our house in the morning before we caught the bus, but today, I was so excited to tell her the news, I wanted to go straight to her house.

"Hurry up Freddie!" I yelled to my brother.

"It's not even time to leave. Why are you rushing me?" he said as he took his time getting dressed.

"I want to talk to Taylor," I pressed.

"Why? You want to tell her that Mommy said, *yes*. I heard you'll talking last night," he replied.

"You are so nosy," I told him.

"I am not nosy, you're just loud. How was I not supposed to hear it with all that screaming you were doing last night?" he asked. "You'd probably be better at cheerleading anyway because you don't do anything but turn cartwheels and dance at soccer," he teased.

"Be quiet boy! No one asked you. Just put your shoes on so we can leave," I fired back.

"No wonder Mommy's always fussing at you in the morning, you are slow as molasses," I teased.

"I may be slow, but I am faster than you," he said as he darted out the door to Taylor and Tyler's house.

"Wait for me!" I yelled as I ran after him.

I rang their doorbell once, and then I knocked on their front door twice, but no one answered. Where are they? I screamed inside my head. I waited a few minutes then I knocked on the door and rang the doorbell again. OMG! What is taking them so long to come to the door? I just couldn't take it!

Just as Freddie and I started to walk away, I heard the door knob rattle and the top lock release. So, Freddie and I ran back to the door. It felt as if it took a million years for the door to open! Unfortunately, it wasn't Tyler or Taylor at the door. It was their older brother, Kris.

"Are Tyler and Taylor home?" Freddie asked.

"No, they had a dentist appointment," Kris answered.

"Are they coming to school today?" I asked.

"I believe so," Kris replied. "Mom didn't give me any reason to believe they wouldn't,"

"Thanks Kris. We'll see you later," Freddie said.

What! Taylor didn't say anything to me about having a dental appointment this morning.

Now I'd have to wait until lunch to tell her the good news.

It was the longest bus ride ever, and the morning seemed to drag on. Every stroke of the clock took an eternity, and it felt as if my teacher would never stop talking. Just 30 more minutes until lunch, but by this time I was agitated and no longer excited about sharing my news with Taylor.

****

Finally!

Just as the clock struck noon, my teacher told us to put away our things and to line up for lunch. It seemed as if we were standing there forever because my teacher was waiting for some of my classmates to stop talking. *"Oh my goodness!"* I thought. *"How many times have we done this? You would think everyone would know by now that our teacher won't let us leave the class until everyone is completely quiet,"*

I bet she was waiting for Devin. He was always running his mouth or doing something he had no business doing. I couldn't imagine or count how many minutes of recess, lunch, and specials we've lost because of him. I wished he would just get his act together!

By the time we made it to the cafeteria it was packed, and Taylor was nowhere to be found. To make matters worse, the lunch line was wrapped around the room. It was going to take me forever to get through this line. I wished I had packed lunch today.

As I stood in the line, I continued to scan the cafeteria. Taylor was nowhere in sight, and I didn't even see Tyler. *Good grief!* How long does a dental appointment take? I totally expected her to be back in school by now.

Just then I felt a gentle tap on my shoulder and heard my name.

"Hi Amira,"

Even before I could turn around, I was fussing.

"Taylor, what took you so......Oh, Hi Kali," I
said, changing my response mid-sentence.

"Well dang on Amira! It's nice to see you
too," she responded sensing I was disappointed
by her presence.

"I am so sorry. Hi Kali. I was just expecting
Taylor," I apologized. "I've been waiting all day to
talk to Taylor and I still haven't seen her,"

"Oh, is something wrong? Did something
happen?" Kali asked.

"No, nothing's wrong," I said, as I continued to search the room. I could tell Kali, but it just wouldn't be the same. Plus, I just wanted to tell Taylor first.

Kali and I made our way through the lunch line. We sat down in our usual spot. There was still no sign of Taylor. We ate our lunch, talked about our weekends, but I really wasn't in the mood for small talk. To be honest, I was too busy looking for Taylor to really listen to what Kali was saying.

"Amira, Amira, Amira!" Kali shouted.

"Huh?"

"Did you hear anything I said?" Kali questioned.

"No, Kali. I am so sorry. I wasn't really paying attention. I guess I was too distracted looking for Taylor," I confessed.

"Well it's time to go and Mrs. Neilson has been trying to get your attention for the past few minutes," Kali said as she pointed to my teacher standing by the door.

I quickly gathered my things and cleaned up the odds and ends left on the table by my classmates because we would miss recess if we didn't clean up after ourselves at lunch.

"Is everything okay Amira?" Mrs. Neilson asked with concern as I got in line to leave the cafeteria. "You seem a little distracted today,"

"Yes, I am fine Mrs. Neilson. I just thought I would see Taylor during lunch," I said assuring her that everything was okay. Lunch came and went and still no Taylor. I guess I am just going to have to wait until recess.

****

Recess couldn't come fast enough. As soon as Mrs. Neilson dismissed our class, I was the first one outside. I made a beeline to our favorite spot, but there was still no sign of Taylor.

I sat on the bench and I waited. Within minutes all my friends joined me at our usual spot.   Kali, Sarah Bell, Tyson, Xavier, Jonathan and my brother Freddie. They were all there. All of them except Taylor.

"Have you seen Taylor and Tyler?" I asked Freddie.

"Nope, I guess they're still at the dentist," he responded.

"What in the World! This is the longest dentist...," I began to complain.

"Amira, Amira! What did your mom say?" Taylor shouted as she ran towards me eager to know.

"Yes, Yes, Yes! She said yes!" I screamed. Immediately forgetting how frustrated I had been waiting for Taylor to arrive at school.

"Yes! I am so excited! We are going to be cheerleaders!" She squealed as we jumped up and down hugging each other in the middle of the playground as if no one else mattered.

"When is our first practice?" I asked with anticipation.

"Tonight!" Taylor answered.

Her answer was like a dagger to my heart! I have soccer practice tonight and I knew my mom would not let me skip it. We'd already had that conversation!

"Oh, I won't be able to come tonight," I said with my head hung low with disappointment.

"Why?" She probed.

"It was part of the deal," I sighed.

"Deal! What deal?" she asked confused.

"The deal my mom and I made for me to participate in cheerleading," I told her.

"What?" she repeated.

"Yes, soccer has to come first! I can't miss any practices or games. If there is a conflict soccer is the priority," I told her as I recapped the terms and conditions of my agreement with my mom.

"Really!" she responded with dismay.

"Yup. If soccer and cheerleading practice fall on the same night, I must go to soccer. If the games are at the same time on Saturday, I have to go to my soccer game first," I explained. "The same thing goes for Girl Scouts. That was the deal,"

"I guess something is better than nothing," Taylor concluded.

"Yup. I am just grateful she said yes," I agreed with a sigh of relief.

CHAPTER 3

I can't believe it! I finally get to go to cheerleading practice tonight. Between soccer and Girl Scouts, I've missed four cheer practices and two games since my mom agreed to allow me to cheer. It seemed like an eternity.

I asked my mom if we could leave a few minutes early so that I would be guaranteed to get there on time. My mom tends to leave only in enough time for me to arrive on time, but this time I wanted to be early.

"Mommy, what time is it?" I asked.

"5 o'clock," she replied mindlessly.

"What time is practice?" I asked.

"6 o'clock," she replied.

"What time are we leaving?" I asked.

"Amira!" she huffed. I could tell she was becoming annoyed, but I am just so excited I can't help myself.

"Amira," she repeated. "If you don't stop harassing me, we aren't going to go. We will go when we go, and if you ask me another time, we won't go,"

Cheerleading practice couldn't come quick enough and the only reason my mom was taking me was because Ms. Dee had to work late. While I waited, I did a double check of my bag. Sneakers, check. Water, check. Snack, check. I hope this is everything, I really want to be prepared.

"Amira," my mother called from her bedroom.

"Yes," I replied with anticipation.

"Go get Taylor so we can go to practice," she instructed.

"Yes, ma'am," I answered already halfway out of the door.

Taylor and I talked the whole way to practice. Although this was my first official practice, Taylor had been teaching me the cheers after school. The team had already learned five cheers, and I didn't want to be too far behind.

By the time we arrived at practice, most of the girls were already there warming up. We weren't late, but we weren't early either. My mom left in just enough time to be a few minutes early, but not so early that we would have to wait.

Ms. Dee hadn't arrived yet, but the assistant coach Ms. Dominique was there. She was short. I was almost as tall as she was and, as a matter of fact, I was taller than all the girls too.

Taylor said Ms. Dominique was a dance teacher and, *"didn't take no mess,"* She was all about discipline and technique. *"Form and formation,"* she reminded us throughout practice. When we forgot the routine, it was laps, burpees and planks. I had no clue what a plank or a burpee was, but by the time we got mid-way through practice I became an expert at both, so much for easing into my first day at practice.

By the time Ms. Dee arrived we had already gone over our first five cheers a million times. I know that is an exaggeration, but it felt like a million and it was certainly too many to count, and when Ms. Dee arrived it didn't get any better. This was a lot more than I expected. I didn't realize I was going to work so hard at cheerleading practice, but I was loving every minute of it.

"Okay ladies, it's time to learn our halftime routine," Ms. Dee directed. "1,2,3,4...5,6,7,8, turn, step, jump and hold,"

I was so confused, I didn't know my right foot from my left, and it seems everyone was getting it except me.

"Keep up Amira, you have a lot of time to make up for," Ms. Dee demanded. "Again, 1,2,3,4... 5,6,7,8, turn, step, jump and hold,"

"Yes, ma'am," I replied exhausted. However, I knew I had to keep up and learn the routine. Quitting was certainly not an option, especially after I'd begged my mom to let me participate. I didn't really want to quit, but I was tired and I could use a break. This was more work than soccer, even when we are running drills and scrimmaging the entire practice time.

"Okay ladies, water break," Ms. Dominique said.

"Thank you, Jesus!" I exclaimed. I couldn't believe how exhausted I was, and practice wasn't even close to being over.

Making The Squad

As we sat down to drink our water and eat our snack, Taylor started introducing me to some of the girls on the team. "Hey y'all, this is Amira," Taylor announced. "Amira, this is Zahla, Kennedy, and Hayden,"

"Hi, Amira," they all responded in unison.

"Hi, everyone," I replied. "Is practice always like this?" I asked.

"Yep, pretty much," Kennedy replied.

Kennedy was tall, but not quite as tall as I me. She was also a little heavier than the rest of the girls. You would think that she would struggle because of her size, but it was just the opposite. Kennedy was out dancing all the girls on the squad, aside from Zahla.

Zahla is Ms. Dominique's daughter, and she and Hayden were the most petite girls on the squad. But Zahla had one of the biggest personalities on the team. Zahla could dance and tumble. She was also at the top of all the lifts and pyramids. She was also quite vocal the entire practice, trying to tell everyone where to go and what to do. *She seemed a bit bossy to me.*

"All right ladies break time is over. Let's get into formation," Ms. Dee commanded. At the sound of her voice we all sprang to attention.

"Okay, from the top," she instructed. "1,2,3,4…5,6,7,8, turn, step, jump and hold," she counted.

1,2,3,4…5,6,7,8, turn, step, jump and hold, I counted to myself. All right, I think I've got it! Maybe it was the break because it feels like I am doing much better. Well, at least I am not tripping over my own feet anymore. For the remainder of practice we rehearsed our half-time routine, and by the time my mom returned I had it down pat. Practice hadn't quite ended, so my mom stood on the sidewalk talking to the other parents.

Making The Squad

"All right ladies bring it in," Ms. Dee said, just as the sun began to set. "Much better, but some of you still need to make sure that you practice on your off days. If you don't know the routine by Saturday, you'll be sitting on the sidelines with your parents. I have recorded the routine and I will email it to your parents for you to practice so there are no excuses. Do you understand?" she asked.

"Yes ma'am," we responded in unison. I don't think anyone would have responded negatively, even if they hadn't understood! I know I wasn't going to. I was just going to go home and make sure I practiced that routine.

CHAPTER 4

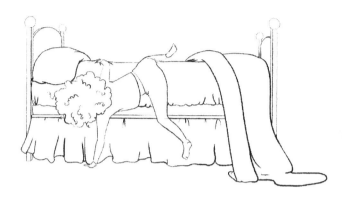

"Ughhhhhhh..." What in the world! It felt as if every muscle in my body had betrayed me as I attempted to roll out of bed the next morning. I had never been in so much pain! My legs were stiff as boards as I walked into the bathroom to get ready for school. Thank God, the hot water from the shower loosened up my muscles just enough to get dressed.

"Good Morning, Amira," my mother greeted me.

"Good Morning, Mommy," I groaned.

"You look like you've been run over by a truck. Are you okay?" she inquired.

"Well that's because I feel like I've been run over by a truck," I grunted. "Every muscle in my body hurts. I had no idea that cheerleading practice would be this exhausting. We moved the entire time,"

"Yes, Ms. Dee and Dominique were pushing you girls hard," Mommy added as she made my plate.

"You're telling me," I agreed as I opened the refrigerator taking out the juice. "Ugggggh, this feels like it weighs a hundred pounds," I gasped as I put the container on the counter.

"You might want to stretch before you go to school today," my mother suggested. "You know you have soccer practice this afternoon, and if you don't stretch, you're going to feel it later,"

Stretch? How in the world am I going to stretch? I barely had enough energy to brush my teeth this morning, let alone walk down the stairs to the kitchen table to eat breakfast.

"If it's too much, I can talk to Ms. Dee about you just waiting until next year to cheer," my mother suggested.

"NO!" I shouted.

"Excuse me, young lady," My mother stared at me as if I had lost my mind.

"Um, I mean no ma'am. I am good. I got this," as I straightened up to signify that I wasn't in that much pain.

"Good Morning!" my brother Freddie said as he kissed my mother and slapped me on the back before he sat down to eat breakfast.

"Ouch!" I shouted in agony. "What is wrong with you boy? You need to keep your..."

"Hey!" my mother cut me off before I could finish my rant. "Freddie keep your hands to yourself and Amira stop being so dramatic,"

"But mom!" I pleaded.

"Enough, I don't want to hear another word. The two of you need to finish your breakfast and get out of here to catch the bus," she said, ignoring my pain as she nursed my baby brother Ellis.

I shoved the rest of my food in my mouth as I got up from the table, grabbing my backpack to walk out the door.

"Um, excuse me," mom said, clearing her throat as she stopped me in my tracks. "Can I get some suga?"

Reluctantly, I turned around, walked back to the table and kissed both my mom and my brother Ellis good bye.

"Amira," she said as I walked back towards the door.

"Yes, ma'am?" I answered.

"Anything worth having is worth working for," she said.

"Yeah, I know Mommy," I responded.

"Amira, one more thing," She paused waiting until she had my full attention. "Stop letting your brother get you all worked up. You know he's just trying to work your nerves to get your attention,"

"I know Mommy, but sometimes I am just not in the mood," I whined.

Without saying a word, she put my brother Ellis down, stood up and walked towards me, then she picked me up and gave me a big hug of reassurance.

"Thank you, Mommy," I said trying not to let the tears fall.

"You're welcome baby. I love you," she reminded me. "Now get out of here before you miss the bus,"

By the time I got out of the house, the bus was pulling up to the bus stop and I had to run to make it. Being the last person on the bus at the last stop gave me very few seating options. So, sitting with Taylor was out of the question.

Giving the bus a quick scan, I realized that my options were slim to none, so I sat at the first empty seat available. I dropped my bag, laid my head back against the seat and closed my eyes in defeat. This was not how I'd expected to start my day.

****

The rest of the week didn't seem to get any better. It took my body three days to get adjusted, so every day I woke up in pain. I walked around in pain and practiced in pain. I think my face was frozen in a permanent frown and I am sure my attitude wasn't any better, but there was one thing for sure, I was ready for Saturday's game.

"Amira get up. we have a busy day," my mother said as she nudged me out of the bed.

"Ugh," I groaned as I rolled over pulling the blanket over my head. It had been a long week and I didn't want to get out of bed. Between school, Girl Scouts, soccer, and cheerleading practice I was exhausted, and as much as I wanted to cheer at today's game, I didn't want to get out of the bed. So, I laid there wishing time would rewind just a little bit, so I could get a few more minutes of sleep.

"Amira!" my mom yelled from the hallway. "Get out of the bed, get dressed, brush your teeth, wash your face, and go down stairs so you can eat your breakfast, and I can comb your hair!" she ordered as I finally rolled out of the bed.

"And don't forget to bring your bag with your cheerleading stuff. We must leave directly from the soccer field to get you to the football game on time. You will just have to change in the car," she reminded me.

"Yes ma'am," I groaned again, as I dragged myself to the bathroom.

By the time I had finished getting ready and gone down stairs to breakfast, my food was cold. "Great," I mumbled under my breath. This is one of the few times my Mommy had cooked since my baby brother, Ellis, had been born, and it had taken me so long to get dressed, my food had gotten cold.

I knew I must be moving slowly. Freddie had finished his food and he was always the last one at the table. *"Get yourself together girl,"* I tried to encourage myself and prepare myself mentally for the day.

Making The Squad

"Hurry up Amira! I still have to comb your hair," Mommy hollered from the family room, rushing me.

"I am coming Mommy, I just have to finish my food," I responded.

"We need to leave the house in 5 minutes, so you won't be late for your soccer game," she insisted.

"Okay," I said as I shoved the last of my eggs and bacon into my mouth. I cleared my plate from the table and went to sit in between my mother's legs.

My mother brushed my hair into a quick afro puff, and we were out the door.

Finally! I was so excited I could jump out my skin. My first game! My first game as a cheerleader! My soccer game couldn't end fast enough. although we'd won, and I'd scored two goals and blocked two more. Standing there with the cheerleaders was really where I wanted to be. We were a little late getting here because all the soccer games were running behind, but at least I made it to the field as the game began.

"Get into formation Amira!" Coach Dee instructed. "Don't worry about warming up, I am sure you're still loose from your soccer game,"

"Yes ma'am," I said as I raced to my spot.

"Ready, set," Taylor called out to start the cheer.

"Okay!" We all responded in unison.

"Move! Move! Get out of our way, get out of our way! Because the Panthers are here, and we are ready to play!" It was our first cheer and we rocked it.

I was so excited I couldn't stop smiling, you couldn't tell me anything. I was a cheerleader, and nothing felt better. By the time halftime came we were winning 14-7 and I was ecstatic about performing our halftime routine.

We lined up and pranced our way across the field. We got into position and the music started. When we started dancing the other team's crowd erupted in applause. We performed the halftime routine that Coach Domonique choreographed to perfection, and by the looks on the other squad's faces, they had no idea that we would be dancing, and their performance couldn't come close to anything that we had done. We danced our hearts out. All that work had paid off and it felt great! As we walked back across the field with our heads held high our faces were beaming with pride. Well at least I know mine was!

Our team won 21 – 7. By the end of the game I had been bitten by the cheerleading bug. I just knew I was going to do this for the rest of my life.

"That was soooooo much fun!" I squealed to Taylor.

"We killed it!" Taylor shrieked. "Did you see the look on the other team's faces when we started dancing? They had no idea we were going to do all of that!"

"Okay, ladies huddle up," Coach Dee called. "Good job today, but don't get too comfortable. We must finish out the season and get ready for competition. Practice on Monday. Hands in,"

CHAPTER 5

The rest of the season was more of the same: school, soccer, girl scouts, and cheerleading. Except now as we were closer to the end of the season, Coach Dee and Coach Domonique added another practice. So instead of just two days a week, we were now practicing three days a week. Thankfully, the added practice was on Sunday and it was just right next door at Coach Dee's house, otherwise I doubt my mom would have let me go.

She was already complaining about all the practices and activities between my brother and sister with daddy being in and out of town with travel for his job. "I will be glad when the season is over," she complained every time something else was added to the calendar. I could tell it was starting to wear on her because she also worked on the weekends doing photo shoots and selling her books at festivals and expos.

"I can't be everywhere all the time," she complained. "Why does the football schedule keep changing? I have missed half of your games this season because of scheduling conflicts. They really need to get their act together over there. Don't they know we have other things to do?"

Every time she started to complain, I would make a silent exit because I knew she wasn't really talking to me, and I didn't want to make the situation worse by saying something silly. It was more about her not being able to make all the games. My mom just liked to be there no matter how much she fussed.

****

We had worked hard all season, and to be honest, I was exhausted. Between cheerleading, soccer, girl scouts, and school I was running on empty. Although I loved cheerleading, it was taking a toll on me and I think it was starting to show. I was literally dragging myself to practice.

Come on Amira, get to your spot!" Coach Dominique barked. "Ladies, do I need to remind you that if you are not on point, you will not perform? We've been doing this too long to be making these types of mistakes,"

"The competition is two weeks away and we have to be tight and right!" Coach Dee added.

"I know it's tough, but we have a reputation to uphold. We are the Panthers!"

"Let's do it again," Coach Dominique demanded. *"5, 6, 7, 8!"*

We must have gone through that routine at least 1000 times. I thought practice would never end. My legs were so numb I could barely move them, and I thought my arms were going to fall off. It felt like the first day of practice all over again.

"Huddle up ladies," Coach Dee said. "I know you have been working hard this season, and my adding this competition has made our season extra-long, but we don't want you to think that your hard work has gone unnoticed. So, this weekend we are going to enjoy some rest, relaxation and pampering,"

Pampering, what's that? I could use the rest and *Lawd knows* I needed to relax, but I had no idea about *pampering.* However, if it had anything to do with rest and relaxation, I was all in!

"This weekend we're going to do a little team building at the Moca Princess Day Spa," Coach Dee added.

Did she say Moca Princess Day Spa? I have been asking my mom for months to go to that place. My friend Kali went for her birthday last year and she talked about it for weeks nonstop. She said it was beyond awesome and she'd really felt like a princess.

"We are going to meet on Saturday at 3 o'clock," she continued.

Saturday? Saturday? My mom was not even going to be in town on Saturday! She had a book event in Richmond. I knew my dad wouldn't be able to take me because he will be home alone with all of us. He'd be watching football in the basement all day.

How disappointing. I thought as I walked back to the house from practice. I could not believe it! *"Uggh,"* I groaned as I dropped my cheer bag when I came through the front door.

"What's wrong with you?" my mom questioned.

"I can't believe it!" I whined.

"Believe what, Amira?" Mom asked, becoming less patient.

"I can't believe I won't be able to go to the Moca Princess Day Spa with the team," I whined.

"Oh, girl, Bye!" Mom responded, dismissing my agony.

"I'm serious mom. The whole team is going to the spa on Saturday, and you won't even be here to take me," I groaned.

"And?" she responded.

"And, I really want to go!" I pleaded.

"Who said you weren't going?" she inquired.

"No one. But you are not going to be here, and dad is probably going to be watching football all day," I responded.

"And what does that have to do with you going to the spa with the team?" she asked again. "There you go jumping to conclusions. I have already paid for you to go and you're going to be riding with Coach Dee. So, what are you whining about?"

"Ummmmm. Nothing. Thank you, Mommy!" I said as I hugged her as tightly as I could. "I love you Mommy,"

"I love you too. Now go take a shower. You stink!" she said swatting my bottom as she continued to prepare dinner.

Making The Squad

****

OMG! SPA-A-A-A-A-A DAY! I can't believe it's finally here! I have been looking forward to this day all week long. I must have asked Kali at least 1,000 times what to expect.

"Enough already, Amira! You will see when you get there," she told me.

I just couldn't help myself. no matter how many times she described it to me, it was *w-a-a-y* better than I could have even imagined. When we pulled up to the building there was a huge sign in the window that said, *"Go Panthers!"* That alone made my day, but there was more. When we walked in it was like something in the movies. There were purple and pink sparkles everywhere.

"Welcome ladies!" Our host greeted. "Please go to the dressing room and change into your robe and slippers,"

"We get robes and slippers?" Taylor squealed. "Are we supposed to take off our clothes too?"

"No silly! Just your jackets and socks and shoes," Coach Dee responded.

I was glad Taylor asked, because I was thinking the same thing. I knew when my Mommy went to a spa, she said that she gets completely undressed to get her massage! *Oh well. I guess we were not going to get massages.* After we took off our coats and put our socks and shoes in the locker our host took us to the make-up station.

"We're getting make-up!" I said as I looked at Coach Dominique.

"Yes, girls. Not only will you be getting make-up today, but you will also be getting a manicure and pedicure.

"Manicure and Pedicure? What's that?" Zahla asked confused.

"That's when they paint your fingernails and toenails," I answered. "I got one when I went to the nail salon with my mom,"

"All right! I already know what color I am getting. It's going to be green on my toes and yellow on my fingers," Zahla announced.

"Slow your roll ladies. They need you to pick out your eye shadow and lipstick first," Coach Dee said. "Relax we will get to all of that later. Enjoy the moment. You all have worked hard this season,"

And I did exactly that. I sat back and relaxed. I was here to be pampered and I deserved it. For my eyes, I chose a sparkling purple, and for my lips, I chose a hot pink. To top it all off, the make-up technician added a little pixie dust all over my face to give it a little

something extra.

While we were getting our make-up done,

the host brought everyone their own goblet of

strawberry lemonade, with a straw of course, so

we wouldn't mess up our lip stick. *Goblet* is just a

fancy word for glass.

When my make-up was finished, I was

escorted to the manicure and pedicure station.

There were 10 pink oversized puffy chairs in a

row. Each of them had their own soaking tub for our feet. When I sat, my attendant pressed buttons on a remote control and suddenly the water started to bubble, and the chair started to vibrate. Although the other girls were chattering excitedly, I just laid my head back, closed my eyes, and enjoyed the moment.

OMG! This is the life. I could do this every day. I am sure I fell asleep as the attendant filed my nails, massaged my hands and feet and polished my nails. I chose purple for my hands and blue for my toes. After all, we are the Panthers, and I had to represent our team colors. As an added treat they said that we could get a design on our fingers or toes.

When my nails were completed, I just sat there with my eyes closed absorbing it all. I was so relaxed I fell asleep, and I think I even started snoring.

"Okay, Amira you may go to the next station," my attendant said as she gently tapped me on the shoulder to awaken me from my slumber. *Slumber* is just a fancy word for *sleep*, that a princess uses. And today, I am a princess.

"There's more?" I asked surprised.

"Yes, there's more," she added.

"Well then, lead the way," I responded.

"Okay Ladies, now we're going to make lotion," our host said.

Squeals and gasps from the team followed. I am sure mine were the loudest. I love making lotions! I do it all the time at home with my sister Aukema, although Mom says we're just making a mess!

Today I am a princess, and I am making princess lotion with shea butter, bees' wax and almond oil. I have no clue what any of this stuff is, but it sure feels and smells good. I think Mom will like this lotion.

Spa Day has been the best day ever! Kali was *so* right. No matter how many times she tried to explain it, I had to experience it for myself. The make-up, the manicure, and pedicure. if this is pampering, *then sign me up for every day*.

"Okay Ladies, it's time to go," Coach Dee announced.

No-o-o-o-o-o-o-o-o! Does it have to end so soon? I am not ready to leave, not yet. I need more pampering.

"Coach Dee," the host interrupted.

"Yes," Coach Dee replied.

"Can the girls do a cheer before they go?" she asked.

"Yes ma'am!" she replied with her southern twang.

"Panthers," Coach Dee called.

"Yes ma'am," we answered in unison.

"Form and formation,"

And without hesitation we all stood at attention.

"Ladies we have been asked to cheer," she announced. "Are you ready?"

"We are always ready!" We answered in unison.

There were just some things we were conditioned to do and answering Coach Dee and Coach Dominque was one of them. We were one squad and one voice, so when our coaches called, we all knew they were talking to one team and we answered accordingly.

"Move!" she said. With no other instructions we sprang into action.

"Move, Move, get out of our way! Get out of our way! When the Panthers are here, we are ready to play!" We executed the *Move* cheer, and then performed two more cheers. When we finished the spa erupted into applause. Not only were the staff applauding, but the other guests and parents were applauding too.

"You all are great!" the host complimented. "If you cheer anything like this for the competition, you will be sure to win," she continued with confidence.

"Well thank you darling. we certainly expect to," Coach Dee declared. "Thank you for being such a gracious host. Our girls have really enjoyed themselves. However, it's time for us to go so we can get ready for tomorrow,"

"You're welcome, anytime! We will be happy to host your victory party," the host replied.

"Well start planning ladies, because we will certainly be back to celebrate our success," Coach Dominque declared with confidence.

CHAPTER 6

It's competition day and we are ready. We

have been practicing for months, and we have a

brand-new routine. We are stepping, flipping,

lifting, doing pyramids, cheering, and dancing. If

the other teams thought our halftime routines

were something before, they were about to be

blown away by this new routine. Coach

Dominique had outdone herself.

Making The Squad

I had ridden with Coach Dee to the competition because we had to be there two hours early. My family would be coming later. It was a bit much to have everyone out of the house before 8:00 for a competition that didn't start until 10:00. we were still unclear about our actual time of performance. By the time we got to the gym, it was already packed. There must have been at least 20 teams competing, and the winners would not be announced, nor trophies awarded, until the end, so we knew it was going to be a long day.

Before the competition began all the teams had to meet in a smaller gym away from the larger gym where the competition would be held. The teams were organized by category and age. We weren't the youngest team in the competition, nor were we the oldest. So, we were placed in the Juniors Division. This group included teams with girls ranging from ages 6 to 9.

Next, the director went over the rules of the competition and explained some general *Housekeeping* Rules. *Housekeeping is just the dos' and don'ts for the day*. After the announcements, all the teams used the time to get in one last rehearsal, including us, The Panthers.

After about 15 minutes, the director came back into the small gym to let everyone know their place in the line-up. The minis would go first, followed by the juniors, then the intermediates, and then finally the seniors. Each division had about four or five teams and we had no idea what the other teams were like because we had to wait in the smaller gym until it was our turn to perform. That meant we wouldn't see any of the other teams in our division perform because we were performing last.

The wait was nerve-wracking. We could hear the reaction of the audience but had no idea what was happening.

Making The Squad

"How do you think we are going to do?"
Taylor asked as we stretched in preparation of our
routine.

"We'd better win, considering how hard we
worked," I answered. "I don't know about those
other teams, but I know we are on point and
every single one of y'all better bring it!"

"I am so nervous," Hayden said.

"Me too," Kennedy added.

"I think we are all a little nervous," Zahla replied.

"I just can't believe Journey won't be performing," Taylor noted.

"Well, what do you expect? She was never at practice and she barely knew the routine," I reminded Taylor.

"I know, but I really didn't think that my Mom and Coach Dominique would bench her," Taylor continued.

"Well from what I understand, the parents had a meeting and the coaches reminded all the parents that if their girls couldn't make it to practice then they couldn't participate in the competition," I repeated from the conversation that I overheard that I wasn't supposed to have been listening to.

"But it's still a shock," Taylor said.

"Taylor, you shouldn't feel sorry for her because she would have just messed up the routine again. Don't you remember when she dropped Zahla at the game because she hadn't been to practice to really practice our lifts?" Kennedy reminded her.

"Hmmm. You don't have to remind me," Zahla recalled. "It took weeks for my wrist to heal,"

"Well, I am just glad she still showed up to support us," I noted. "I didn't think her Mother would bring her after all of the drama with the birthday invitations,"

"Please don't bring that up again. We need to focus our energy on positivity," Taylor said with an expression, as if she had been sucking on a sour lemon.

"Yes people, let's focus on the positive. Circle up!" I said.

As the girls gathered around for our pre-game prayer and pep chant, I looked at Taylor and gave her hand a slight squeeze. I am so glad she encouraged me to ask my Mom if I could be a cheerleader. Without a word, Ms. Dee gave me a huge hug acknowledging my gratitude.

Soon after we finished praying, Coach Dee and Coach Dominique came back.

"Okay ladies! It's show time! This is what you've been working for all season. Make sure you to leave it all on the floor," said Coach Dominique.

"Form and formation!" Coach Dee shouted. And with that one command, we all stood at attention and stepped into the gym chanting:

"Dale City Panthers, Cheer, Cheer. Dale City Panthers, Cheer, Cheer. Dale City Panthers, Cheer,

Cheer. We are the mighty Cheer Panthers from Dale City,"

We chanted until we got into our places and immediately the gym erupted. I don't think anyone expected us to be stepping. Especially not anyone in our age group. After our step introduction, we moved into the cheer part of our routine with our parents placed strategically throughout the crowd cheering along with us, it made our cheer that much more impressive. After the cheering component we went right into our dance routine without missing a beat. We ended the routine with an amazing tumbling pass.

The sound of the crowd was deafening. It seemed like the audience was cheering from the time we stepped on the floor, to the time we finished. I don't know what those other squads did, but I don't recall the applause for the other teams being this loud. With our chest heaving in exhaustion we pranced off the floor to our designated seats in the bleachers. Now all we could do was wait until the trophy ceremony.

****

We were on pins and needles as the older girls performed. I don't recall seeing anything spectacular to be honest, and I truly believe our routine could have beat some of the older girls, although only time would tell.

As the final team performed, the competition organizers asked all the teams to come to the floor for the awards ceremony. With nervous energy, our squad sat quietly, while gripping each other's hands so tightly that our fingers became numb. There were actually only three teams in our age division, so everyone was going to get a trophy, but there was only going to be one winner. I hoped and prayed it was going to be us.

"In 3rd Place," the judge began, and my stomach dropped. *"The Dale City Cowboys,"*

The crowd applauded as the Cowboys stood to receive their trophy.

"Our 1st runner up," the judge continued, wasting no time. *"The...Dale City...Redskins,"*

The crowd erupted, and I immediately began to cry. *How could we have lost? I know we* were *the best and we worked so hard this season!*

"Why are you crying Amira?" my mother said smiling with excitement.

"Because we lost," I hung my head.

"Amira! What are you talking about? You didn't lose," Mom tried to console me.

"Yes, we did! The Redskins got 1st," I sobbed.

"No, Amira. They didn't get 1st, they got 1st runner up. Which means they got second place. your team won 1st place," she explained.

"What! Well, why didn't she just say that?" I quickly dried my tears and got up to join my team on the podium to get our championship trophy.

Middle School

CHAPTER 7

Throughout elementary school, everything was pretty much the same. Cheerleading and gymnastics in the fall and winter, clinics in the spring and trying to convince my Mom to send me to cheer camp during the summer between our family travels. By the time I reached middle school, I was more than ready for a change of pace and a new challenge. Middle school was supposed to be much different than elementary. We would have an opportunity to cheer for two seasons, football in the fall, and basketball in the winter. And we would be able to travel to different schools across the county.

The first year of middle school as a 6th grader I didn't waste time trying to figure out when tryouts would begin! I made sure I got a copy of the schedule. I needed to make sure I had all the information before asking my parents for permission to participate.

"Tryouts are next week, Tuesday, Wednesday, and Thursday after school from 2:30 -5:00. The games start in mid-September and go through the end of November. We practice on Mondays and Tuesdays and games are on

Wednesdays," I explained to my parents before they could ask a question.

"I don't know Amira. It seems like a lot, *especially* with the demands of your Science and Math Program. Don't you think it would be a good idea to wait until next season to tryout, so you can get a better feel of the program?" Dad suggested.

"NO!" I shouted, mortified by his recommendation. "I mean, I can handle it Daddy. Aren't you the one who always tells us, '*Be balanced with academics and activities?*'" I bargained with his own words.

"Well, I guess you got me there," he laughed. "Using my own words against me. That's a great one Amira, maybe you should consider being a lawyer," Dad joked.

"Lawyer or not, academics come first. And if your grades are not on par, I will snatch you right off the team," Mom warned with a stern face.

"Yes, ma'am," I promised as I kissed them both on the cheek after they signed my permission slip.

****

"Did your mom sign your permission slip?" I asked Taylor as we stood waiting for the bus.

"Absolutely! I made sure it was the first thing she did when she came home from work yesterday," she assured me.

"You're so lucky Taylor," I told her.

"Why?" she asked a little confused.

"Your parents never give you a hard time about participating in stuff," I responded.

"Are you *kidding* me! My Mom always asks me 50,000 questions and Dad's first response is always, *NO*," she said setting the record straight.

"I just don't participate in everything under the sun like some people I know," she said looking directly at me, as if I do too much. "So, it's a little easier to get a, *yes*, when I ask for something.

"Me? I don't do a lot?" I responded pointing to myself acting as if I were offended.

"Really, Amira! Between cheer, school, gymnastics, choir, acting and singing lessons. You make me tired, just thinking about all you're doing," she reminded me as she ran down the list of some of my activities. "I am just surprised that your parents can keep up with everything they do, *and* everything you, Freddie, Aukema and Ellis have to do too!"

I hesitated for moment knowing that every word she said was true. "Well, I guess you're right. Maybe I shouldn't be complaining about my parents giving me a hard time about trying to participate in another activity,"

Making The Squad

After we boarded the bus, I just sat in
silence really thinking about what Taylor had said.
Maybe I am doing too much. But whether I am or
not, I am not about to give up cheerleading. So, I
turned in my permission slip as soon as I got to
school.

The rest of my day was spent navigating my
way through the hallways as I changed classes
throughout the day. Middle school is way
different from elementary school. There is no
lining up at the door when it's time to change
class, and there is no teacher escorting us
everywhere we go! In middle school, students are
completely independent and responsible for
getting ourselves to class on time.

CHAPTER 8

After school I was exhausted, but my day was far from over. I still had to do my homework, go to gymnastics, and clean the kitchen. After all, today is Tuesday. my day to do the dishes and clean the kitchen.

Last year my Mom assigned Freddie and me days to clean the kitchen, before that, Aukema had to do it every day. Now I totally understand why she used to complain so much. Cleaning the kitchen is the last thing I want to do after a day like today, but I knew better than to complain.

I grabbed a snack from the refrigerator, *"Fruit first,"* I could hear my mother saying. She didn't mind us having a snack when we got home from school, but she always wanted us to select fruit first. And then, if we were still hungry, we could get something else from the pantry.

When I finished my snack, I sat at the table navigating the maze of homework from all my pre-advanced placement classes. Most of my teachers emailed our assignments, and all our work had to be submitted electronically. There could be no *the dog ate my homework* excuses. Also, you couldn't use, *I left it on the bus, or I forgot it at home*.

I was sitting at the table, for what seemed to be only five minutes, before Mom announced that it was time for me to go to gymnastics. When I looked at the clock, two hours had already passed, and I wasn't even halfway done with my homework. I quickly put my things away and grabbed my bag. I knew today was going to be busy, so I made sure to get my things together before I left for school.

I love gymnastics, and outside of cheerleading, it is my favorite sport. Cheer and gymnastics really go hand and hand. There is no doubt that you're at an advantage if you know how to do somersaults and stunts as a cheerleader. My gym ensures that we are well-trained and prepared.

I was on the mat when I saw Taylor come running through the door. Taylor is always rushing to practice. She goes to her tutor after school, and by the time she finishes, she barely has enough time to make it to practice on time.

"Slow down Miss Jackson!" Coach Kookie yelled from the other side of the gym. "You're going to hurt yourself bursting through those doors like a wild boar!"

"Yes ma'am," Taylor respectfully replied, as she slowed her pace to a fast walk towards the locker room.

"Take your time Taylor. There is no need to rush, practice hasn't even started," Coach Kookie reassured her.

"Yes ma'am, but I don't want to be late," Taylor explained.

"You're fine Taylor. Your mother has already informed us of the change in your schedule, and she let us know that you might be cutting it a little close," Coach Kookie explained.

"All right everybody! Let's warm up," Coach Kookie said as she re-directed her attention to the rest of team.

Taylor had changed and was in and out of the locker room before we could take our places on the mat.

Miss Taylor Jackson! Get your little narrow hips up from the mat until you've stretched properly. We are too close to competition and we don't want any unnecessary injuries because you didn't take the time to stretch," Coach Kookie scolded Taylor.

We all giggled.

"Yeah Taylor, you know you need to stretch," I teased. "You know stretching is important," I repeated, although I hated stretching myself. Sometimes I held the same stretch for minutes, only pretending to stretch as I talked it up with my teammates.

"Thank you Amira, but I got this," Coach Kookie said.

Everyone giggled even louder.

****

"It's almost time to go and I want us to go through the routine one more time before we call it quits. You look great team, but we need to make sure to synchronize our tumbling passes. and make sure our stunts are precise," Coach Kookie instructed as we did an about-face and made our way back to the mat.

"I am not sure if my stomach can handle being tossed in the air one more time!" Hayden whined. "We have gone over this routine five times already. So that means I have been tossed, thrown and flown in the air over 20 times in the past 2 hours. *Can a Sistah get a break*!"

Immediately the entire team erupted in laughter.

"What? What?" Hayden questioned trying to figure out what was so funny.

"'*Can a Sistah get a break?*' Really Hayden?" Kennedy mocked her. "You are the only non-Sistah here!"

"Psssh!" Hayden popped her lips. "I'm yo' sistah! As long as we've been rolling together, I better be your sistah! Y'all betta be my S I S T A H S!"

"Absolutely," we all agreed without hesitation because we knew if anyone would have said anything different, Hayden would have been hurt to the core. We also agreed because we all knew that despite her race, Hayden was really our "sistah," From that very first year, she was one of us. Even after she moved to another part of town, she insisted her Mom put her on our team.

"All right, all right. *Sistah, brotha, Mama, Daddy, or Cousin.* I need y'all to get on the floor and nail this routine," Coach Kookie commanded bringing us back to the task at hand. "Let's get through this, and you can have your family reunion later," she said laughing at her own joke.

"Come on Hayden. you can do it," Zahla tried to encourage her.

"I know I can do it," Hayden snapped. "But I am just tired!"

"Don't be snapping at me Hayden, Sistah or not, I am not the one!" Zahla warned her as she started walking towards Hayden.

"Oh no. This cannot be good," gasped Taylor attempting to grab Zahla's arm, but it was already too late. Before Taylor could grab hold of Zahla, she was already half way across the mat standing nose to nose with Hayden.

I knew these two little firecrackers. neither of them was going to back down. So, I knew I needed to act quickly before it went farther downhill.

I am assuming that Kennedy had the same thought, because we simultaneously leaped forward attempting to separate the girls. As I reached for Zahla and Kennedy took hold of Hayden, I stepped on Kennedy's foot and rolled my ankle. Then I heard it snap!

I fell to the ground immediately, screaming in agony, as I rocked back and forth. The pain I felt in my foot was indescribable.

I screamed, "Don't touch me! Don't touch me!" As all my teammates came running to my aid.

"Are you okay Amira? What happened?" Coach Kookie asked as she ran to my rescue making a path through my teammates.

"I think it's broken! I think it's broken!" I screamed at the top of my lungs.

"Kennedy, call 911. Taylor, call Mrs. Fuller!" Coach Kookie directed as she elevated my leg and quickly assessed my injured foot. "You're going to be okay Amira," she tried to reassure me as she kicked into first responder mode. "Zahla, go get some ice!"

Within minutes my mother came running through the doors. She must have been waiting in the car or on her way to pick us up.

"What happened Mir, Mir?" she asked as she came running towards me with my little brother, Ellis, in tow.

"I stepped on Kennedy's foot and I think I broke my foot!" I explained as the tears poured down my face.

"What in the world? Let me have a look at it," she insisted as I flinched at the thought of anyone touching my foot.

"Don't Mommy! It hurts so bad," I cried as my mother started to examine my foot.

"Try to calm down Amira. Help is on the way," Taylor assured me as the sirens of the ambulance filled the background.

"I am so sorry Amira," Kennedy apologized as tears began to well up in her eyes.

"It's not your fault Kennedy," I said to relieve the guilt I could see on her face as tears streamed down her face.

"See what y'all did," Kennedy screamed as her sadness became rage and she re-directed her attention to Zahla and Hayden. "Y'all were in here acting a fool, and Amira has broken her foot tryin' to stop y'all from fighting. Now, she won't be able to do the routine in the competition! She just can't be replaced!"

Routine! Competition! I hadn't even thought about the competition. When I heard Kennedy's words, I just dropped my head onto my knees and sobbed.

When the paramedics arrived, they stabilized my foot and whisked me away to the hospital.

I spent the next three hours in the emergency room getting x-rayed and fitted for my cast. My foot *was* broken, in the worst possible way. The emergency room doctor explained that I might need surgery, so she was putting the foot in a cast to prevent any further damage.

I stayed home for the next two days because the pain medication made me extremely sleepy and my mother said that I would be hopeless at school. By Friday, my mother had scheduled an appointment with a podiatrist, a doctor that specializes in treating feet.

CHAPTER 9

"Yep, it's definitely broken," Dr. Binni announced after he reviewed my x-rays. For the next few minutes Dr. Binni explained the type of break, the upcoming surgery, and the time he anticipated I'd need for recovery. "It's going to take about a year to heal completely,"

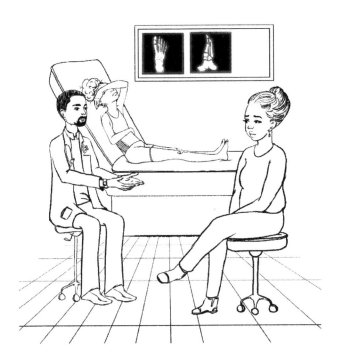

"Did you say a year?" I repeated. I snapped out of my haze.

"Yes, a year between the surgery, rehab, and healing. It will be about a year,"

I looked at my mom in panic as the tears began to roll down my face. "A year. A year MOMMY! I won't be able to cheer, dance or do gymnastics for a year! Not only am I missing the competition, I won't get to cheer my first year in middle school! What am I supposed to do?"

Grabbing my hand to console me, my mother tried to reassure me that everything would be okay.

"Amira, you are going to be okay. Your foot is broken and there's nothing we can do to change what happened," she said.

"Amira, let me clarify. We are going to do your surgery next week. After your surgery you will be in a cast for two months. Then, we will remove your cast to check your progress. If everything goes as expected, we will put you in a boot for a month. After this you will start your rehab. You should be back on your feet and in the gym within the next four to five months. However, you will still need a few more months to allow the foot to heal completely," Dr. Binni, tried to comfort me too.

Unfortunately, his words were of no comfort at all, and although the process was just as he described, the first five months of school were nothing like I imagined.

I spent the next three weeks following the surgery at home recovering with a tutor. When I finally made it back to school, I felt like a complete outsider. I didn't know anyone in my classes, and to make matters worse, I missed the competition and I wasn't on the cheerleading squad. Taylor and the girls tried their best to make sure that I felt included by inviting me to the practices and games, but it just wasn't the same.

Every day I went to school I felt totally alone in a sea full of people. Every day was the same. Get up, go to school, go to class, get out of school go to rehab, leave rehab go home and study. I spent the rest of my time staring out the window of my bedroom crying. The only time I would leave my room was to go to the bathroom or to go to eat dinner.

I'd sit at the table shoveling food down my throat and quickly excuse myself to avoid any unnecessary conversation. After a few weeks my routine wouldn't fly with my parents anymore.

"Amira, your Father and I would like to talk to you when you finish the dishes," Mom announced.

"Yes ma'am," I replied, as if there was any other option. When I finished the dishes, I found my parents cuddled up on the family room sofa.

"You wanted to talk to me?" I asked as I came into the room announcing myself.

"Yes Amira. Have a seat," Dad said and moved his feet off the chaise to make room for me.

"How are you doing?" Mom asked.

"I am fine Mommy. Why do you ask?" I said trying to sound as normal as possible.

"Because we've noticed that you have been spending a lot time in your room. You've been snappy with your brother, and none of your friends have graced our doorstep in weeks," my mother noted.

"I am just tired. Middle school is different than elementary school. There is so much more work. I am just trying to focus on my work, and besides, there isn't really anything I can do with my friends with a broken foot," I responded attempting to convince my parents and myself. But I knew it wasn't the truth. I wasn't doing anything in my room, except crying. I'd been ignoring the hundreds of text messages and phone calls from my friends begging to come over. I had also begun avoiding my friends at school, acting as if I didn't see them in the hall, and purposefully going in the other direction when I saw them coming my way.

I couldn't explain it to my parents because I didn't understand it myself. It was just different. I felt invisible, I didn't fit in, and I didn't feel connected. My classes were filled with people I didn't know, and I only saw my old friends as I passed through the halls on the way to the next class. I even sat alone at lunch. I was sad, and alone, and I didn't understand why.

"Amira, we understand that you are going through a lot right now, and you are devastated about not being able to cheer or to do any of the other activities you've always done, but this is just temporary. Your foot won't be broken forever. You will be back to normal in no time, doing the things you enjoy," Dad said trying to reassure me.

"Your Daddy's right Amira. This is just temporary and although you can't do everything you use to, you can do some of the other things you enjoy, but just didn't have time to do before because you were so busy with cheer, dance, and gymnastics. You have so many gifts, and you are super talented in so many ways. Maybe you should think about what will make you happy in the meantime," Mom said to encourage me.

"I am HAPPY!" I snapped back at her remark so fast I didn't have time to adjust my tone.

My mother just looked at me. I knew *that* look. Snapping back at her would get me smacked into tomorrow.

"Well you don't sound happy, you don't look happy, and you are certainly not acting happy! As your parents we are concerned. we just wanted to check in with you," she responded in a very calm tone, which let me know she knew that I had lost my mind for a split second and she was going to let my indiscretion slide.

"I am fine Mommy. Really," I said once more.

"Okay, Amira, but if you need to talk, we are here," they reminded me.

"May I be excused?" I requested.

"Yes, you may, but I need some sugar before you go to bed, and don't forget to say your prayers," Mom said as she stood up. "I love you Amira," she said as she took my face into her hands. "I know you are dealing with a lot and this has been difficult, but remember, you are more than a conqueror, and you can do all things through Christ who strengthens you,"

She kissed me gently on my lips, hugged me a little longer than she did normally, and excused me to my room.

CHAPTER 10

When I woke up the next morning, I was exhausted. I had prayed and cried all night. I felt broken, not just my foot, but everything. Everything in my life felt broken. I had no clue how I was going to fix it. So, I tried to put on a happy face, just the same.

After I got dressed and got my things ready for school, I went downstairs for breakfast. I forced myself to be extra nice to Freddie. I loved on Ellis as much as he could stand and engaged in small talk to demonstrate to Mom that I was okay. The ride to school was quiet, but as soon as I got out of the car, I dropped the act and pressed my way to class.

"You know she is not buying it," I could hear Freddie yell from behind me.

"Buying what! What are you talking about?" I snapped as I stopped walking.

"You know, that fake act of you being happy. She knows you are just doing that to keep her off your back. Do you think she is really buying it?" he asked.

"I have no clue what you are talking about NOSY! I am happy!" I insisted to my brother who was really starting to work my nerves more than usual.

"Come on Amira. Are you really going to try to convince me, of all people? You are not happy. you're miserable! All you do is sit around in your room crying. I am your twin brother. We shared a womb. We have been rolling tight since inception. When God created you, He created me. So, I know you. You think I don't notice when something is wrong with you? Just because I don't always say something, doesn't mean I don't know or don't care. I have watched you for weeks walk around here feeling as if you're defeated because you broke your foot and you can't do the things you have always done. But that's not the end of the world! Did you really think that you would be a cheerleader for the rest of your life? Eventually you are going to get old, and you physically won't be able to do that stuff anymore" he stated.

"Well, I am not old right now, and I want to be a cheerleader and to do the things I have always done," I barked.

"You're missing the point Amira. Like Mommy and Daddy said, you are more than just a cheerleader," he responded.

"Do you think that you would be able to bounce back so easily if something like this had happened to you? What if you'd broken your hand, and you couldn't play baseball? Would you be happy? Would you be walking around whistling, *"Oh Happy Day*?" I think not. You would be devastated. So yes, I am devastated and if I need a minute to get myself together, give me a minute to get myself together, Dr. Phil," I fired off.

"I get it, but it's been more than a minute. It's been more like two months," he said as he hung his head. He knew in this moment there wasn't much more he could do or say. I had dropped the mic and I limped away.

****

School was monotonous, every day like the day before...so was my afternoon routine. However, today when I got home things were a bit different. It was just Mommy and me. Daddy and Ellis were gone and Aukema and Freddie weren't home from their after-school activities.

I wasted no time going to my room. As I began to hop up the stairs, my mother called out from the kitchen, "I want you to do your homework downstairs today,"

"Ma'am?" I asked a bit confused.

"I want you to do your homework down here today. Your laptop is on the kitchen table. You can do your homework and keep me company while I cook dinner," she asserted.

"Yes, ma'am," I hesitated as if I even had an option to refuse her request.

When I went into the kitchen the food smelled *s-o-o-o-o* good. It looked like my mother was cooking a Thanksgiving feast. What in the world is going on? She never cooked this much, especially not during the week, and it looked like she had made everyone's favorites including mine. There was fried chicken, collard greens, macaroni and cheese, yams, black-eyed peas and rice, oxtails, ribs, grilled salmon with pesto, green beans, and stuffed peppers! There was enough food to feed about 30 people.

"What are you doing Mommy?" I couldn't resist asking.

"Cooking dinner," she giggled.

"I can see that Mommy," I noted. "Why are you cooking so much food?"

"Oh, we are having guest over for dinner. Your Daddy invited a few people over. Would you like to invite anyone? We have plenty of food," she offered.

"No, I am good," I refused.

"Not even Taylor?" She suggested.

"No, I am good Mommy. I think she has a game or something," I assumed as I tried to move on. I really wasn't in the mood for company and the way I have been avoiding Taylor over the past few months, she probably wouldn't accept my invitation anyway, despite the fact she loves to eat.

"Okay, suit yourself. When you finish your homework, clear and set both tables for dinner," she instructed.

How am I supposed to clear and set the tables with a broken foot? Of course, it was just a thought. *I wasn't going to let those words fly out of my mouth. I am crazy, but not that crazy.* So, I did just as my mother instructed. I finished my homework, then cleared and set the table. Just as I was finishing, I could hear the garage door opening. It was the rest of the Fuller crew, Daddy, Aukema, Freddie, and Ellis. I assumed Mommy had sent Daddy to pick up Freddie and Aukema, and to the store by the looks of all those bags in his hands.

"Amira, come help put this stuff away," My dad called.

Really! Now he's expecting me to help with the groceries? Don't they understand that my foot is broken, and all this stuff is just extra? I could be up in my room chillin' right now. But again, these were just thoughts, and not words that would ever depart from my lips when talking to my parents. So, I did and said what any child in their right mind would say when her father asked her to do something despite her affliction.

"Yes, Daddy," I complied. While I was helping to put away the groceries the doorbell rang.

"I'll get it," my mother hollered, as she made her way to the door with Ellis in tow.

Although Ellis is bigger now, he is always in my mother's arms.

When my mother opened the door all I could hear was a flood of voices. They all sounded familiar, but the one voice really stood out. My Pop-Pop's. You always knew when Pop-Pop would enter the room. He was always loud and full of laughter. I couldn't quite make out who the other people were, but it sounded as if there were a lot of them. I really wasn't in the mood for people today, so I had made up in my mind that I would excuse myself as soon as I finished dinner. I thought, "Thank God it's not my turn to do dishes,"

There was a steady stream of people for the next 10 to 15 minutes. By the looks of our house, we were having a family reunion. I sat in the chair next to the doorway listening to everyone talk while trying to avoid any meaningful conversation myself. Then the doorbell rang again. How many people did they invite?

"Amira get the door!" my mother shouted.

Is she serious? What is this? Make Amira work day!

"Yes ma'am," I responded and moved without hesitation, despite my thoughts.

When I opened the door all my friends were standing there: Taylor, Zahla, Kennedy and Hayden. I was in shock and I couldn't do anything, except just stand there. I had been avoiding them for months, and now they were standing in front of me face to face.

"Are you just going to ignore us like you've been doing for the past few months or are you going to let us in?" Kennedy demanded.

I was speechless. I didn't know what to say or do. I also couldn't figure out why they were here.

"Umm, oh yeah. Come in. What are you doing here?" I asked a little confused.

"Your Mom invited us over for dinner. So, you know if your Mom is cooking, I am eating," announced Taylor giving me a gentle nudge as she took off her shoes at the door.

"She did?" I asked with confusion. Why would she invite my friends over in the middle of the week for dinner?

"Yes, she did!" Kennedy answered. "Do you have a problem with that?"

"No, of course not. It's good to see all of you," I responded.

"Well that's hard to believe seeing how you haven't returned any of our text messages or phone calls since you broke your foot," Kennedy recounted the obvious.

"I am sorry guys. I just have a lot going on," I attempted to apologize.

"It's okay, we get it," as Zahla reassured me that they understood.

I hadn't really seen or talked to the girls since I broke my foot. I pretended that I was asleep when they tried to visit, and I ignored their texts and calls.

"Hello Ladies," Mom greeted everyone as she peered around the corner. "Dinner is done and we will be ready to eat in a few minutes.

"Yes ma'am," they all responded in unison followed by giggles.

"Come have a seat," I said as I guided the girls into the kitchen, and we sat around the island. "Would anyone like something to drink? Water, Kool-Aid, juice?

"Amira," Hayden whispered as she leaned in close.

"Yes,"

"I am really sorry that we caused you to break your foot," she apologized.

"It's okay Hayden. It was an accident," I said.

"I know, but I still feel so guilty that Zahla and I were the cause of your injury," she apologized again. "It was just so dumb the way we were going at each other for no reason,"

"I am sorry too. We never meant for anyone to get hurt," Zahla added.

"Thank you for apologizing. It means a lot," I said, accepting their apology half-heartedly, but not really forgiving them. Because of them, I'd broken my foot, missed the competition, and couldn't try out for the school team.

"We brought you something," Taylor interrupted as she ran back towards the door. "We have been trying to give it to you for weeks, but we haven't had a chance to because we haven't seen you," she said throwing just a little shade. Taylor came back into the room with a huge bag.

"Where did that come from? I didn't see you bring anything in," I said.

"My Mom brought it with her when she came in behind us," she said with a smile. I didn't even see Ms. Dee and Mr. Omar come in.

"What is it?" I asked with excitement, trying to figure out what was in that huge bag.

"Well we just brought you a little something, something from the competition. We hope you like it," Kennedy said.

"Girl if you don't hurry up and open that bag!" I hollered with anticipation.

"Okay, Okay!" she said as she reached in the bag pulling out a humongous trophy.

"We won, we won!" They all squealed at the top of their lungs. "And although you couldn't be there, we wanted you to have this,"

In that moment I was so overwhelmed that I broke down into tears. I was filled with emotions. I didn't know what else to do. I was excited that our team won, I was sad that I couldn't be there, and I was speechless that they had given me the trophy.

"What's wrong Amira?" Taylor asked as she hugged me gently trying to comfort me.

"Nothing, thank you for thinking of me," I sniffled. "It's just a lot. I am just sad because I really wanted to be there, but I am so happy that you all thought of me,"

"Of course, we thought of you Amira. We couldn't have done this without you always pushing us for perfection," Zahla added as she came over to hug me too.

"Well that didn't go anything like I expected," Kennedy blurted out. "I certainly didn't think that you would be over here crying. I thought this would make you happy,"

"It does make me happy. I am just going through a lot right now," I tried to explain as I dried my tears, and put on a happy face.

"Well you don't sound happy and you certainly don't look happy," Kennedy reiterated.

"Girls, time for dinner," Mom announced as she walked into the kitchen. "Go wash your hands so we can say grace,"

Thank you, Jesus! My mother's timing was perfect. Knowing Kennedy, she would have forced me to talk and to be honest. I am just not ready.

CHAPTER 11

There must have been over 30 people at our house last night. Although it was fun seeing my friends and family, I was both physically and emotionally exhausted. I woke up moving a little slower than normal, but I knew I had to press on. It had been months since I had talked that much or been around that many people.

After I finished getting dressed, I went downstairs to breakfast. Freddie, Daddy, and Ellis were already seated at the table eating a combination of leftovers Mommy had transformed into a breakfast feast: Salmon cakes with rice, eggs, bacon, grits and toast.

"Good Morning Amira," Mom almost sang.

"Good Morning Mommy and Daddy," I said as I kissed them both. "Good Morning big head," I said to Freddie, as I nudged his head. "Morning

Thuc, Thuc," I said as I kissed Ellis on the forehead and sat down at the table in front of the huge championship trophy.

"That's a big trophy," my mother noted as she put my plate in front of me.

"Yes, it is," I said not really giving it too much attention.

"It was really thoughtful of them to want you to have it," she added.

"Yes. I guess so," I responded. I am not sure how thoughtful it was, but it was a huge reminder of the fact that I couldn't go and be a part of the competition. That I can't be a part of the squad now and I am not a part of the team. I hadn't earned that trophy. *It wasn't mine,* but I knew that it was no need to explain that to my mother because she wouldn't understand. So, I finished my breakfast and waited patiently at the door for my Father to take us to school.

"Everyone locked and loaded?" my Father asked before we pulled out the driveway.

"Yes, Daddy," I responded, not amused by his stale joke.

"Okay. Well let's pray," he replied. And in unison we recited the Lord's Prayer as we did every morning before leaving the house:

> *"Our Father who art in heaven, hallowed be thy name. Thy kingdom come, thy will be done, on earth as it is in heaven. Give us this day our daily bread, and forgive us our trespasses, as we forgive those who trespass against us. And lead us not into temptation and deliver us from evil. For thine is the kingdom, and the power, and the glory, for ever and ever Amen,"*

My family said this prayer daily.

"Amira," Dad said.

"Yes, Daddy?" I answered still half in a daze.

"Forgiveness can be more beneficial for the person who is forgiving than the person who needs forgiveness,"

"Uhh... What does that even mean?" I asked totally confused by his statement.

"Well sometimes people really can't move on until they learn how to forgive the person who's hurt them. You were hurt because of someone else's actions, and you may be feeling angry, sad, confused or even resentful, wondering why you. But until you really forgive them in your heart for the pain that they caused, you really won't be able to move on," he stated.

"Ok, Daddy," I agreed so I wouldn't draw out this pointless conversation any longer. I had already told the girls that I accepted their apology. What more did he want me to do? No matter how many times they apologized, it wasn't going to change the fact that my foot was broken, and my life has come to a complete standstill.

"Accepting someone's apology is different from forgiving someone," he said, as if he were reading my mind.

"Yes Daddy! I understand," I said as I attempted to jump out of the car before it came to a complete stop.

"Amira, I know you want me to stop talking, but you could at least give me some sugar before you go to school," he pleaded.

"I'm sorry Daddy," I said as I leaned back into the car to give him a kiss.

"I forgive you Amira," he laughed trying to prove a point.

"Not funny Daddy," I said closing the door behind me.

As I went into the school, I became extremely irritated trying to figure out how I was supposed to act. I didn't understand why everyone was so concerned. I am fine. What do they expect me to do? Am I supposed to be rolling around on my knee scooter doing a happy dance? I have broken my foot, and it's totally depressing not being able to do the things that I love. So, forgive me if I am not happy all the darn time.

The conversation with my dad really puts me in a funky space. However, I did my best to be cordial and not avoid my friends. When I saw them coming down the hallway I didn't go in the opposite direction and when they spoke, I spoke back. It was mentally exhausting, but I did it. By the time I got home I really didn't want to be bothered with anyone and I attempted to make a beeline straight to my bedroom.

"Not so fast young lady. I want you to do your homework down here, and when you're finished, I want you to help me finish dinner," my mother instructed.

"Yes ma'am," I answered with the only realistic response I could give. When my mother asked me to do something, I really didn't have a choice in the matter. It was almost 9:00PM before I got to my room. Homework had turned into dinner preparation, which ran over into dinner, which ran over to dishes, that ran over to playing

with Ellis and helping him to get ready for bed.

The only thing I wanted to do when my

head hit the pillow was to go to sleep. However, I

couldn't get comfortable because something was

poking me in the back of my neck. I lifted my

head to find the source of my annoyance, there

was an envelope beneath my head.

It had my name on it written in marker with

squiggly lines all over. *"What in the world!"* I said

to myself as I opened the letter and began to read.

> *Dear Amira,*
>
> *I know you are going through a lot right now and I just wanted to let you know that I am here for you. We have been best friends since kindergarten, and I hope that you know that you can talk to be about anything. We used to spend every day together and now we hardly see, talk to, or text each other.*
>
> *I miss you and love you more than you could ever know.*
>
> *Love, Taylor*

By the time I finished reading the letter I was in tears. Every day for the next two weeks it was the same thing. I'd spend the entire afternoon and evening with my family and then going into my room to find

another letter.

CHAPTER 12

I had to admit I was growing accustomed to and looked forward to getting the letters of encouragement every day. Although I still felt very alone, the letters made me feel as if someone cared. They were a huge distraction from just staring out the window crying. I read the new ones and re-read the old ones every night. I especially loved reading the letters from Mommy that were sprinkled in every three to four days. They weren't always letters, but words of encouragement and scriptures reminding me that I was more than just a cheerleader.

Her notes reminded me that:

"I was fearfully and wonderfully made,"

"I could do all things through Christ,"

"Faith without works is dead,"

It was those and other reminders that I received daily that gave me the courage to ask Mom for help. I had been feeling hopeless since I'd broken my foot and I wanted out. So, I mustered up the nerve to go talk to my Mother.

When I walked into her bedroom, she was organizing her closet. "Excuse me Mommy, can I talk to you for a minute?" I asked as she re-folded and stacked her t-shirts.

"Yes, what is it?" she responded without turning around.

"Well first I want to say thank you for all the letters of encouragement. They really mean more to me than I have words to express," I said.

"Oh, you're welcome Sweetie. I figured you could use a reminder of how many and how much people really care about you," she said.

"Yes, I guess they really do," I responded solemnly. "When did you have time to go around and collect all those letters?"

"I didn't,"

"Huh?" I was a little confused. If she didn't collect them how had they gotten here?

"Remember when we had the big dinner a few weeks back? Well I had asked everyone to write you a letter or words of encouragement to help you push through this difficult time,"

"Oh," I said as I thought back to that evening. I hadn't seen anyone bring in a note. "I didn't even notice,"

"Well I am not surprised. You haven't noticed very much lately," she said as she looked at me through her closet door.

"Oh, okay," I spoke slowly, not sure how I was going to ask my mother for help. "Mommy...," I paused, and she waited patiently for me to speak. "I haven't been feeling so good

lately," I continued.

"What's the matter?" she asked as she

walked through the closet back into her bedroom

and stood next to me.

"Do you have a fever, a headache, or

stomach ache?" she asked all in the same breath

grabbing my hand.

"No, it's nothing like that," I assured her.

"Well what hurts?" she asked looking into my eyes.

As tears began to pool in my eyes, I took a deep breath and tried to collect my thoughts so that I could explain how I was feeling.

"Why are you crying?" My Mother asked with concern as she hugged me tightly. "Whatever it is, it's going to be okay,"

"But I am just so sad, and my heart is so heavy, it hurts," I sobbed in my Mother's arms.

"Why are you sad Amira?" she asked as she held my face in her hands drying my tears.

"I don't know exactly, but ever since I broke my foot things just haven't been the same and no matter what I do, it's just not getting better," I cried.

My Mother just sat there and allowed me to cry. I am not sure where the tears were coming from because with all the crying, I've done over the past few months I thought I didn't have any more tears to cry.

"It will be okay Amira. Let's pray," she said without hesitation. She prayed aloud:

> *"Right now, in the name of Jesus, we are lifting Amira up in prayer.*
>
> *She needs Your healing power. Heal her heart, heal her mind and*
>
> *heal her body, for Your Word says, "'We are healed by Your stripes.'"*
>
> *Now give us guidance and direction to get her the help she needs to*
>
> *be restored. Amen,"*

My mother prays about every situation and I didn't expect this situation to be any different.

"Thank you, Mommy. I have been praying too, but it doesn't seem like God is hearing me," I cried some more.

"He hears you Amira and He will answer your prayers," she reassured me. "Let Mommy make a few phone calls and we are going to make sure you get the help you need,"

"Okay Mommy," I said as I dried my eyes. "Thank you for praying for me,"

"Absolutely! I pray for you daily and I am just so grateful that you had the courage to come and talk to me. I know that you have been struggling and I wanted to give you your space, but as your mother I knew something was going on," she acknowledged.

"I sort of figured when you started making me do my homework downstairs and all the letters started appearing on my pillow," I confessed.

You know they say that *"Confession is Good for the Soul," and it certainly worked for me*. After I finished talking to my mother it felt as if a huge burden had been taken off my shoulders. I knew she was going to help me figure out what was going on, and she was going to make sure I had what I needed to fix it.

CHAPTER 13

Sure enough, the next day after school I had an appointment with Dr. Ross, a family therapist and a longtime family friend. She and my mother have been friends since my older sister Aukema was a baby. So, when I arrived at her office, there were lots of hugs and kisses that I am sure other patients didn't receive at their visits.

There was some small talk between my mom and Dr. Ross, but my mother made a quicker than usual exit.

"I am going to get out of here so that you and Amira will have all the time that you need," my mother said as she hurried out the door.

"Come into my office Amira," Dr. Ross said guiding me in from the lobby.

"Yes ma'am," I said as I followed her down the hall into a very fancy room at the end of the hall. This didn't look like any doctor's office I had ever been in. There was not an examination table, scales, tongue depressors or flash lights to inspect your ears, eyes or nose. Instead, there was a plush soft pink sofa, two emerald green lounge chairs, matching throw pillows, beautiful accessories, and some amazing art. She even had prints by some of my mother's favorite artists, like Racheal Scotland, Frank Morrison, and Albert Fennell.

"Have a seat Amira," Dr. Ross offered.

I scanned the room quickly trying to decide exactly where I should sit. I reclined on the sofa and I rested my head on the pillow. I'd seen someone do that in a movie.

Dr. Ross chuckled a little and said, "You don't have to lie down Amira. We can talk sitting up,"

"Oh," I responded feeling really embarrassed.

"No worries. You're not the first person to do it," she assured me. "I have a sofa for couples and family therapy," Dr. Ross sat in the adjacent chair, put on her glasses and took out her notebook.

"So, tell me what's going on,"

I paused for a moment because I had no idea where to start, and to be honest I didn't even know what was really going on. I didn't have the words to describe my feelings.

Not breaking the silence, Dr. Ross sat patiently waiting for me to respond. I sat a few more minutes as tears began to well up in my eyes. Then finally I just said it.

"I am just sad," I sobbed. "I don't know why. I want to be happy, but it just seems like all the things that used to bring me joy I can't do anymore,"

She waited again as I wiped my eyes and nose with the tissue that sat on the coffee table.

"I broke my foot over the summer right before school began, and I missed the first few weeks of school recovering from surgery. I have been in physical therapy for the past three months. I couldn't tryout for the cheerleading squad, I couldn't go to nationals, and I can't do gymnastics or dance. I can't do anything," I explained in between my tears.

O-M-G, it was like someone had opened the flood gate and everything came rushing out. I must have talked for hours. I told her about my loneliness, my mood swings, and my total lack of interest with anything to do with my friends. I told her how I resented them for causing me to break my foot, although I knew it was an accident. It made me feel a certain kind of way about them being able to go on with their lives while I sat home alone and broken.

I talked a lot and my emotions rolled from sadness, to anger, to fear, and back to sadness again. When I finished, she gently took my hand and told me it was going to be okay. She told me that she was going to ask me some questions that would help her better understand what we needed to work on moving forward.

When she finished, I asked, "So, what's wrong with me?"

She smiled and responded, "Nothing's wrong with you Amira. You are showing signs of *Stress Response Syndrome*, and what you are experiencing is totally normal given what you have dealt with over the past several months. However, as you get older you must learn how to manage obstacles and navigate and overcome the challenges. Up until now, your parents have taken on the responsibility of making it better.

They have kissed your boo boos and made all your worries go away with lots of loving hugs and kisses. I am sure if they could make this go away, they would certainly try. However, as you get older and things don't go as planned, you must learn how to make things better for yourself. You have had a very traumatic injury and it has completely changed your life as you knew it. All the things that you thought made you who you are, are now gone, and it has rocked your world. When you broke your foot it altered you physically, emotionally and cognitively,"

"Uhm," I thought. I have no idea what that word means.

"Excuse me Dr. Ross. What does "*Cognitive*" mean?" I asked.

"I'm sorry Amira. "*Cognitive*" is a word used to describe how you think. It's how your brain processes and applies information," she explained.

"Oh, Okay. I guess that makes sense," I said.

She chuckled again and continued her thoughts. "So now what we have to do is equip you with the tools you will need to manage the unexpected and stressful situations. We also want to work on removing the self-doubt and negativity,"

"Okay! What do I need to do?" I asked feeling super eager to fix me. Just talking to Dr. Ross already made me feel 100 percent better, and I was more than willing to do anything she suggested.

Dr. Ross smiled and said, "You are so much like your mother,"

"I hope that is a good thing Dr. Ross?" I asked.

"It's a very good thing Amira. I am going to give you one homework assignment and you can bring it back the next time you come. Just complete the evaluation and try to be as thorough as possible. It may seem a little repetitive but try to answer all the questions," she instructed.

"Oh. I am coming again?" I asked a little surprised.

"Yes. We are going to have a few more conversations if that's okay with you?" She asked.

"Yes! Absolutely Dr. Ross. I really enjoyed talking to you," I assured her.

"Great. I look forward to our next visit," she said as she stood up. "I think your mother is waiting for us in the lobby,"

As we walked out of Dr. Ross' office my mother was grinning from ear to ear standing hand in hand with Ellis.

"Were you waiting long Tasha?" Dr. Ross asked my mother.

"No, Ellis and I just walked in," my mother assured her.

"Oh good," Dr. Ross responded. "I gave Amira some homework and explained to her that she is experiencing symptoms of Stress Response Syndrome, and that over the next few visits I will be teaching her some strategies to manage it. I also have some homework for you and Big Freddie. Please read over this pamphlet and let's discuss it at Amira's next visit. "

"Thank you so much. I really appreciate you making the time to talk to Amira," Mom said as she hugged Dr. Ross way too tight.

"Anything for you, Tasha. It was certainly my pleasure," she said as she hugged my mother back equally as tight.

After I left Dr. Ross' office, I wasted no time completing the homework assignment, and that was true for all the other assignments she would give me over the next few months. It wasn't easy and it took some time, but by the time my foot had completely healed so had my heart and my mind.

I had changed my attitude towards rehab, my friends, and the challenges that came my way. My first year in middle school certainly ended *way* better than it had begun. Although I couldn't do all the things I loved because of my injury. I now had the time to do some other things. I joined the drama club, the debate team, and I started taking piano and singing lessons again.

Needless to say, the summer came and went as did my 7th and 8th grade years of middle school. I cheered the next two years and I survived without any other major obstacles. I made some new friends, I tried some new things and I finished in the top 10 percent of my class. I am so ready to go to high school.

High School

CHAPTER 14

By the time I reached high school, I had already been cheering for 7. If I do say so myself, I was pretty good at it, but high school was different. The competition was fierce and tryouts for the team started even before school began.

****

"Mommy, when will we be going back home?" I asked impatiently, probably for the 500th time.

"In two weeks, Amira. Why do you keep asking me the same question repeatedly? The date has not changed," My mother replied.

"Well, tryouts are the week before school begins and I don't want to miss it," I reminded her

for the 500th time," just in case she forgot. "And if
I miss the fall football tryouts, I won't be able to
try out until the winter for basketball season".

"Amira, we will be home in plenty of time
for you to get to the tryouts" she said as she
covered her face with her hat and stretched out
on her beach towel. "Now keep an eye on your
brother Ellis while I take a nap,"

Now don't get me wrong. I love our summer
vacations and we've been to all sorts of amazing
places over the years, like Ethiopia, Paris and
China. I am just thankful to God that we weren't

half way around the world this summer. We stayed closer to home this year because Mom knew I really didn't want to miss tryouts. Last year, when we were in China. It took us an extra week to get home because we missed our initial flight and connections. Mom said we'd take advantage of the opportunity and take a few detours!

But this summer I felt like I was missing out. This was the last year that my old squad would cheer together, and Coach Dee and Coach Dominique had planned all sorts of activities for us all throughout the summer. Most of us would start high school this year. I am sure everyone had plans to try out for their schools' team.

Taylor and I had been texting, calling, and emailing each other all summer. And by the looks of all the pictures she'd sent me, and following them on social media, they were having an amazing summer. I must admit that I was a little jealous. I felt like I was missing out on everything and I think it showed in my attitude. My mom had warned me throughout the summer, "to fix my face,"

"Hey Girl!" Taylor greeted me when I called.

"Hey," I responded with unequal enthusiasm.

"What's wrong with you?" She asked.

"I saw the pictures everyone was posting, and I am just disappointed I couldn't be there," I sighed.

"Girl, are you kidding me? Your family takes the best vacations every year, and you're trippin' because you couldn't go to an amusement park. Please! We can do that again when you get back," She said dismissing my pity party.

"Yeah, I guess so. But I really wanted to be there with you guys this summer" I insisted.

"Really Amira! Not everyone gets to travel across the country or around the world for their summer vacation," she said reminding me how fortunate I am.

"I know, my Mom really wanted us to spend this time together considering that my older sister Aukema, is going to college next year" I said feeling just a little better after Taylor put things into perspective for me. "We've been talking about living in a tiny house forever, and it's cool that it's mobile. But girl it's tight when you're traveling with a family of six,"

"I don't want to even imagine!" Taylor laughed. "When are you coming back?"

"I will be back in two weeks," I replied.

"Perfect! You will be back before tryouts," she said.

"I know, right. My Mom says I'm *harassing* her, asking her the same question over and over again. Then she threatened me. She said if I asked her one more time, I wasn't going to be able to tryout,"

"Girl, you better be quiet. You know your Momma don't play," she warned.

"You know I know," I laughed as we talked about nothingness for at least another hour while I watched Ellis play in the sand.

CHAPTER *15*

Finally! I thought we would never get home. We had been on the road for over four weeks. We made it back just in enough time for me to rest a few days before tryouts, but before we could get in the house good, guess who was at the door?

I was so excited to see Taylor. She has been my best friend since kindergarten. Her family moved in right next door the summer before we started school. What are the chances that a set of boy girl twins, the same age, would live right next door to each other?

I know it had only been two months since we had seen each other between our families' vacations, but Taylor looked different. She had gotten taller, but so had I. She was still very lean and naturally muscular, but she's always been that way. Her hair was in braids, but that was nothing new either. Something was different. I just couldn't put my finger on it as I gave her a quick once over before the squeals and screams began.

We hugged each other tightly and jumped up and down with excitement. We were so excited that we were talking over each other. I am sure neither of us heard a word the other one was saying.

"Okay, tell me all about your summer. Where did you go? What did you do?" Taylor insisted. As she held on tightly to my hands listening.

"Well first we all drove north towards Maine to pick up our tiny house. On the way, we spent a day in Philly and then two days in New York. When we were in Philly, we went to the

African American History Museum and Mother Bethel A.M.E Church, then we visited the homes of Marian Anderson and Paul Robeson,"

"Who are they?" Taylor asked.

Marian Anderson

"Well Marian Anderson was a famous opera singer who performed all over the world but was denied by the Daughters of the American Revolution the opportunity to sing on the stage at Constitution Hall in D.C. because she was black. However, when the First Lady, Eleanor Roosevelt, and President Franklin D. Roosevelt found out about it, they arranged for her to sing on the steps of the Lincoln Memorial. Over 75,000 people came to hear her sing. It was broadcasted to millions over the radio," I told her.

"Wow!" Taylor said. "What else?" she probed.

"Well she was the first African American to perform at the Metropolitan Opera, and she played a big part in the Civil Rights Movement. She became a Good Will Ambassador, and she received the Presidential Medal of Freedom along with lots of other awards. She even lived to be 96," I said impressed with how much I actually remembered, considering I really hadn't wanted to be there. Mom always drags us, kicking and screaming, to things like that.

"She sounds amazing!" Taylor exclaimed. "Who was the other guy you mentioned?"

"Oh, Paul Robeson," I said.

"Yes!" She replied.

"He was also a famous singer and actor who went to Rutgers University on a football scholarship in a city where Mom and Dad used to live. He became a lawyer but didn't practice law very long because of racism. He was involved in the Civil Rights Movement and a part of the Harlem Renaissance," I recalled.

Paul Robeson

"Okay Amira, I know a little bit about the Civil Rights Movement, but I am completely clueless on the Harlem Renaissance," Taylor admitted.

"Don't feel bad Taylor. I didn't know anything about it either before this trip. I mean, I knew about Dr. Martin Luther King, Jr. and Rosa Parks, but I had no idea that it was much bigger than that. The Civil Rights Movement was a non-violent protest to end the segregation of blacks and whites. There were millions of people involved and it included other leaders, some of them even lost their lives because of their involvement, like Malcom X and Medgar Evers. I also learned about Dorothy Height and Fannie Lou Hamer," I shared.

"Well what is the Harlem Renaissance?" She persisted.

"It was the time beginning around the 1910s through the mid-1930s that was a golden age in African American culture from literature, to music, to the stage and art. Icons from that era included Langston Hughes, Zora Neal Hurston, Dizzy Gillespie, Josephine Baker, Ma Rainey and Bessie Smith. Harlem, New York was the place where life and culture transformed for blacks and it helped to form the new black identity after slavery. It was really amazing to see how we accomplished so much and how the things they created still influence people around the world today," I told her.

"That is so cool. Your Mom is always taking you somewhere," she reminded me.

"Yeah I have to admit it was pretty cool. Every place we went, from Virginia to California and back again, she dragged us to some museum or monument. Even though we weren't in school, I sure did learn a lot," I admitted.

"So, when you were in New York, did you go?" She probed.

"To the American Girl Doll Store?" I asked. "Of course, I did. I know I am a little old to still want to go, but I have been wanting to go ever since Aukema went with her godmother a couple of years ago," I recalled.

"How was it? Did you get anything?" Taylor pressed.

"It was better and bigger than I could have imagined. It was four stories tall, and it was more than twice the size of the one at our mall. We spent the whole day there. We had lunch, my dolls went to the salon, and Mom even bought me something after she'd sworn, she wouldn't," I laughed. "It was the best day ever,"

"I can't even imagine. You are so lucky," Taylor chimed in.

"After we left New York, we drove to Boston to see some of my parents' old friends. And of course, we went sightseeing. You know my

Mom. She never misses an opportunity to teach us something, anywhere we go," I said.

"So, how was camp? Who went? What did you do?" I asked changing the subject.

"It was awesome," she sang. "Zahla, Kennedy, and Hayden went. *Guess* who else showed up?"

"Who?" I asked.

"Journey!" she screamed. "I couldn't believe it when I saw her. She was there with the Renegades,"

"Of course, she was. That's the team she went to after she couldn't keep up with our squad," I said. "So, what did she say?"

"Believe it or not, she said that she really missed our squad, and that it was really her Mom who made it difficult for her to make it to the games and the practices. Her Mom really wanted her to be on our squad, but we lived all the way across town, and they could never make it to practices on time," Taylor recounted.

"Oh *really*!" I said in disbelief.

"Yep, and she even apologized to Zahla for dropping her," she said. I shook my head in disbelief as I picked up my jaw off the floor.

"Well what did you all learn? What did you do?" I asked again.

"We did lots of stunts and lots of tumbling. We were so sore when we left that place, we could barely walk. Cheering all day, every day, for a week straight is exhausting," She said. "I have never worked so hard or sweated so much in my life. I think we all lost a few pounds,"

"Guess who else was there?" she added.

"Who?" I asked.

"Coach Courtney," she announced.

Gasping in disbelief, I said "Coach Courtney, the cheerleading coach for our new school? No Way! What was she doing there?"

Shrugging her shoulders Taylor answered, "I have no clue, but she was there all week,"

My mind started racing trying to figure out why she was there. Perhaps the girls who attended camp would have some type of advantage because she had a chance to see what they could do. Taylor and I talked all night because Mom let her spend the night. I couldn't stop thinking about the fact that Coach Courtney was at camp, and that I wouldn't have to same benefit of all that extra practice and training when it came to tryouts.

Taylor ended up spending the whole weekend with me, even though she lived right next door. I think Mom understood how much we missed each other over the summer and how much we wanted to prepare for Monday.

CHAPTER 16

We arrived early to school that Monday for tryouts. School didn't start for another three weeks, but you would have thought school was already in session because of all the students there trying out for all the fall sports. Not only did tryouts for cheerleading start today, but they also started for football, girls' soccer, cross country, and lacrosse. The school parking lot was full.

When we walked into the gym, there must have been over 100 girls. Tryouts were being held for the Freshmen, Junior Varsity, and Varsity squads. As Freshmen, we were eligible to make all three squads. Sophomores and Juniors were eligible for Junior Varsity and Varsity, and Seniors were only eligible for Varsity. The Freshmen and Junior Varsity squads had 15 spots each and the

Varsity squad had 20 spots, so that meant more than half of the girls in the gym wouldn't be making one of the squads. I didn't want to be one of them.

Tryouts were going to go through Thursday, and everyone had to try out, even the girls who were on the team last year. There would be three rounds of cuts. Tuesday evening would be the first cut, Wednesday would be the second cut, and Thursday the final teams would be announced.

The day started with everyone in the same room. The coaches made some general announcements and stated their expectations and the criteria by which everyone would be evaluated. They told us that we would be split into four different groups, and the groups would rotate between each station. Each of us was assigned a number. There were 121 of us. Cuts would be made using the numbers we'd been assigned.

I was assigned number 42, Taylor had number 43, Kennedy had number 78, and Hayden received number 93. I am assuming our numbers were assigned based on our arrival times. The four of us ended up in a different group.

I was in group B and I didn't recognize any of the girls in my group. My group went to the other side of the gym where the mats were laid out. So, I assumed that we were going to be working on tumbling.

"Good Morning girls. I am Coach Lewis and between today and tomorrow you will rotate to all four stations. As you can see, you are starting with tumbling. The other stations are cheer, dance, and stunts and jumps. Here in tumbling we are expecting at minimum, that you can execute a cartwheel and a round off during the tryouts. More advanced gymnastics moves, like back handsprings or back tucks can boost your score. Flexibility is also important, so being able to do the splits will be a requirement as well," she said. "Line up girls,"

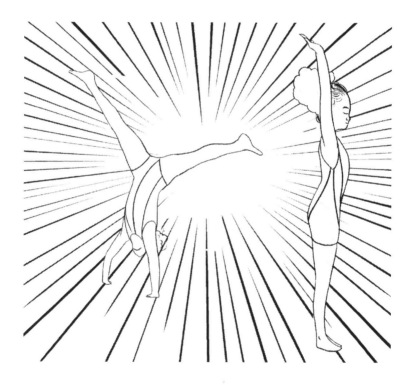

Without hesitation, I was one of the first in line. If I'd I learned nothing else from Coach Dee and Coach Dominique, I'd learned that you lead from the front. We started with cartwheels, both two and one-handed. And right from the beginning, some girls were struggling. How could they come to cheerleading trials and not know how to do a cartwheel? Everyone should know how to do a cartwheel, especially, if they are trying out for cheerleading.

We went from cartwheels, to round offs, to backhand springs, to tumbling passes. There were a lot of falls. I was just glad I wasn't one of them. One girl even fell on her face. I am so glad I'd convinced Mom to put me in gymnastics. I would have hated to have been one of those girls who just couldn't flip.

After about an hour, Coach Lewis asked us to re-assemble.

"Okay girls. Gather up. Some of you have really struggled today. Others of you did extremely well. However, be mindful we are not just making our decision on tumbling. So, if this is an area that you know you don't shine, make sure you do your very best in the other stations. Just because tumbling is not your thing, doesn't mean you're not going to make a squad. It means it's something you are going to have to learn," she assured us. "Your next station will be cheer. You have a 15-minute break, so make sure you get some water and *REPORT ON TIME* to the next station,"

As I was walking to my next station, I saw Kennedy in the hallway. "Hey Kennedy! How's it going? What station did you do?" I asked all in one breathe because I was so excited to see her.

Stopping just long enough to have a quick conversation, Kennedy said "O-M-G Amira! I just came from dance and we had to learn an entire routine in just 30 minutes. Then we spent the next 30 minutes performing in small groups.

Thank God my group performed towards the end because we had some time to practice and get it right. I felt so sorry for the girls who went first because they really didn't have any time to practice. Fortunately, we all performed twice, but you know what they say about making a first impression. *"'You never get a second chance to make a first impression.'"*

"So, how do you think you did? I asked her.

"You know me Amira! I love to dance, so of course, I killed it!" Kennedy said as she walked away strutting her stuff.

"You're so silly! Good Luck! I will see you at lunch," I told her as I made my way to the next station. When I walked into the room everyone was stretching. I wasted no time doing the same. After a few minutes, a really tall, beautiful lady walked to the front of the room. Her skin was like milk chocolate. She wore a big afro. Her teeth were sparkling white with a noticeable gap, just like mine and she stood over six feet tall.

"Good Morning girls. Welcome to cheer. My name is Coach Blanding, and *yes,* I am a cheerleading coach. No, I do not play basketball. And for those of you who are wondering, I am six-foot one inch tall," she informed us in one fell swoop.

I totally knew how she felt. I am five eleven, quickly approaching six feet, and someone asks me every day whether I play basketball. And they are completely shocked when I tell them I am a cheerleader.

"Today we are going to learn three cheers. You will perform these cheers throughout the trials. We will be judging you on accuracy, form, projection, pronunciation, and showmanship. It's not just about whether you can do the cheer. You also have to look good doing it," she said as she directed three other girls to teach us the cheers.

They gave us about 30 minutes to learn the cheers, and then they broke us into small groups. I didn't know any of the girls in my group, but that didn't really make a difference to me, because as my Mommy says, "'I have never met a stranger.'"

"Hi, I am Amira," I said introducing myself to the other girls in the group. Then one by one, everyone else introduced themselves. I didn't know any of these girls because they'd all attended different middle schools. We had a chance to practice for about 15 minutes, and then Coach Blanding started calling up groups.

"Okay girls. I know this is the first day and you just learned these cheers, but it's show time. Let me see what you're working with," she laughed aloud, but more to herself. "Let me see who's going to go first," she asked herself as she searched the room. "You. You girls right in the front," she said pointing directly at me. "Yes, I am talking to you, the tall young lady, with the funky afro puff,"

Everyone giggled, including me, as I looked at my teammates encouraging them to get up as quickly as possible. I was a little nervous going first, but at least we were setting the bar. The other teams were going to have to do better than us or worse than us. As we took our places on the mats, I took a deep breath.

"Ready!" Jada called out.

"Okay!" We all responded in unison, and then we sprang into action. We performed one cheer right after the other, adding transition chants to give us an opportunity to get into our new positions. We added jumps and flips, and we even closed out our routine with a pyramid. It was flawless! Everyone hit their marks, and I thought we came across as a team even though we'd only had 15 minutes to practice. When we finished our routine, it was so quiet you could hear a pin drop. We all looked at each other panting trying to figure out what happened.

"Well girls you certainly put your own twist on things," Coach Blanding commented as we held our final position. "Whose idea was it to do it all as one cheer and add the transitions?" she asked.

Still panting, I explained, "We agreed as a team," But all at once, the other girls all pointed directly to me. I wasn't sure how to receive that.

it almost felt like we had gotten in trouble, and they didn't want to be blamed for adding things. Well that's neither here nor there. That's how I had been taught to preform, and I thought we looked and sounded good.

"Interesting," Coach Blanding remarked. "Thank you, girls. You may have a seat. Let's see who's next," she announced as she scanned the rest of the groups.

One by one each group had an opportunity to perform and everyone had brought their "A game," A few of the squads had added some other elements, and others had done stunts, but I don't think anyone quite delivered like we did. After everyone had finish performing, Coach Blanding released us to lunch.

I quickly grabbed my things and headed to the cafeteria to meet Taylor, Kennedy, and Hayden.

CHAPTER 17

When I arrived in the cafeteria the girls had already started eating their lunch. To my surprise, Zahla had finally made it.

"Hey Girl, where were you this morning?" I asked as I hugged her tightly. I hadn't seen Zahla all summer, and although sometimes we are like oil and water and fought like cats and dogs, I missed her.

"I had to get my physical, and it took forever," she complained. "But my Mom had already called Coach Courtney to explain that this was the only appointment that worked for my schedule. I was only about 15 minutes late, but by the time I arrived you all had already started your group sessions,"

As we ate our lunch, we all re-capped our morning since we were in different groups. We took turns explaining what to expect in each session. I had already talked to Kennedy about the dance session, so I must admit, I zoned out a little bit while she was talking because she tends to be long-winded. However, I was eager to hear what Hayden had to say about stunts and jumps.

"And you know I killed it," Kennedy said as she took way too long to get to what we really wanted to hear. Waiting patiently, Hayden smiled politely as her bestie finished her detailed re-cap of dance. She only began talking when Kennedy stopped talking to take a drink of her water.

"Stunts and jumps were much harder than I expected. Not because I didn't know how, but because everyone trying out isn't as experienced as we are," she explained. "One of the girls in my group didn't know how to spot properly, and she almost dropped me. I guess that's one of the major disadvantages of being the smallest girl in the group. I always end up on top of the pyramid or being thrown into the air," she continued. "But thank God, they had experienced spotters helping us, or I would have been toast!"

"No way!" Zahla gasped hoping that she wouldn't meet a similar fate.

As we finished up our lunch, I told the girls about cheer and how I wasn't sure if adding the transitions and the flips to the routine was a good thing or a bad thing. I acted like it was no big deal, but I had to admit I was a little nervous about what Coach Blanding thought.

The rest of the day went without incident. It was pretty much as the girls described. I totally knew what to expect and I felt completely prepared. At the end of the fourth session, we all came together in the big gym where the coaches re-capped the day and explained that tomorrow would be more of the same.

When the coaches finished talking, I quickly gathered my things so I could meet Mom outside for pick up. Just as I made it to the parking lot, she was pulling up to the door. Taylor and I jumped in as quickly as we could because there were a line of cars behind my Mom.

"How were the tryouts? My mom asked.

"It was tough," I answered.

"It was a lot tougher than I expected, and there were so many girls," Taylor added.

"Well I am sure you all did your best," Mom encouraged us.

"I hope we did. There were a lot of girls and some of them were spectacular," I noted. "I know we brought our A game. I just hope that was enough," I said as I stared out of the window.

There wasn't much conversation after. There was silence the rest of the ride home. My thoughts were consumed with the events of the day. I am sure Taylor's were too. When we pulled into the driveway, Taylor and I said our good byes, and we both just went home. Normally, there would have been a little more chatter, but it had been a long day. I know all I wanted to do was take a long hot shower, eat dinner, and go to bed which was exactly, what I did.

CHAPTER 18

I was awakened the next morning to the gentle nudges from my mother trying to wake me up. "Wake up Amira, it's almost time to go. Your alarm has been going off for the last 15 minutes, and you haven't even budged. We need to leave in about 20 minutes and you still need to brush your teeth, wash your face, get dressed, comb that bird's nest on your head, and eat breakfast,"

Rolling over sluggishly, I dragged myself out of bed. I can't believe its morning already. I'd fallen asleep so quickly last night, that I didn't even have a chance to put together an outfit for the day. So, I quickly grabbed the first thing in my drawer, sprayed my hair with some water and brushed it into a huge afro puff on the top of my head. I didn't have time for anything extra.

I ran into the bathroom, brushed my teeth, flossed, and gargled. I washed my face as fast as I could, making sure to get all the crust out of my eyes, and the dried-up slobber from around my mouth. I had no time for make up or my normal morning routine.

When I finally got downstairs, Mom already had my breakfast on the table, a yogurt parfait, which is my favorite. I love yogurt. It was the perfect breakfast for first thing in the morning for being active.

Before I sat, I kissed Ellis who was sitting at the table throwing Cheerios into Dad's mouth. I spoke to Dad who was desperately trying to get Ellis to eat his own breakfast. I gave Mom a big hug and thanked her for preparing my breakfast and for having it on the table. I was in such a rush that I didn't even notice Taylor until I sat down.

"Oh, Good Morning! When did you get here?" I asked.

"Umm, about 15 minutes ago. I wanted to get here early so we could talk about yesterday, but you were still sleeping. So, you know I had to get me some of that bacon, eggs and pancakes your mother cooked for breakfast while I was waiting," she replied as she took another bite of her bacon.

Taylor and Tyler had been eating at our house for years, so my mom always made extra food just in case.

"I don't see how you can eat like that before tryouts," I said, as I finished my yogurt in what seemed like two bites.

"I can't eat bird food like you Amira. I like a hearty breakfast before I get my day started. I don't understand why you aren't starving by the end of the day," Taylor teased.

"It's not bird food Taylor. It's called healthy eating," I snapped.

"I was just joking Amira. What has your panties in a bunch?" Taylor eased off.

"I am sorry Taylor. I woke up late and I am feeling rushed. I am just a little anxious about today," I apologized.

"I don't know what you're anxious about. Aside from me, you are the best cheerleader out there," Taylor laughed.

"Yeah right! You wish," I giggled. "Enough of the chit-chat. We need to get out of here and I still have to make my lunch,"

"Don't worry, I have already taken care of it," Mom interjected. "You just need to grab your bag and get in the car,"

"Oh, thank you Mommy! I don't know what I would do without you," I said hugging her and kissing her cheek as I grabbed my bag running for the door.

"Yeah, Yeah. Go get in the car. You know how you hate to be late," she teased as she grabbed her keys and headed to the garage. It took us less than ten minutes to get to the school. By the time we got there, they were just opening the doors to the gym. Taylor and I said a quick good bye and jumped out of the car.

"Text me when you're finished," my Mother yelled as I closed the door.

"Okay. Love you, Mom!" I yelled as I ran into the gym.

****

Taylor and I sat towards the front of the gym. It was still early so we started stretching to get ready for the day. The girls started to trickle into the gym: Kennedy, then Zahla, and finally Hayden. By the time everyone arrived, the gym reeked of Ben Gay.

Making The Squad

There were still lots of girls at the tryouts, but the group was noticeably smaller than the day before. I guess tryouts were more than some could handle. I continued stretching and whispered a quick, silent prayer to prepare for the day.

Coach Courtney, Blanding, Newman, and Lewis walked to the front of the gym.

"*Hola, Chicas!*" Coach Newman sang.

"*Hola!* Coach Newman!" we all giggled. For some reason Coach Newman always spoke in two languages, English and Spanish. Although I didn't understand a lick of Spanish, I always understood exactly what she was saying.

"Welcome back ladies. I am glad to see you survived. Today will be like yesterday with one exception. Today we will be making the first round of cuts at the end of the day. As you know, you are being evaluated by our coaches and volunteers. We are not only evaluating your skills, we are also evaluating your character. You are not only cheerleaders, but you are also school ambassadors," Coach Courtney announced. "Being a great cheerleader is only half the job. We are also looking for great people. So be on your "Ps and Qs,"

"All right ladies, please move into the same groups you were in yesterday and go to your assigned station," Coach Blanding instructed. Today Coach Blanding had a head full of butterfly clips in her afro puff, a butterfly bandana wrapped around her wrist, butterfly earrings, and a butterfly t-shirt. It would be safe to say that Coach Blanding loved butterflies.

When we walked into the room, it was set up pretty much the same as yesterday, only there were a lot more spotters in the room. I took a seat in front of the mats and waited for instructions. Coach Blanding explained that we would be working on some specific tumbling passes, and that the spotters would be there to make sure we didn't get hurt. She encouraged us to do our best and to be careful.

As we lined up, I continued to stretch. I wanted to make sure I didn't get hurt or pull any muscles. I wasn't first today, but I was still close to the front of the line. I was standing next to a girl I didn't know, but I'd noticed her yesterday. She was really good. Although she looked familiar, I couldn't quite place her. Momma says, "'If you want to get to know someone, introduce yourself.'" So, I did.

"Hi, my name is Amira," I said extending my hand.

"I know who you are Amira," she replied.

"You do!" I responded surprised. How does she know me? I tried to remember where I could have met her.

"Yes, Amira! *I am Karis, Karis Penderson*," she announced.

"Karis, Karis Penderson," Why does that name sound familiar? I repeated it, trying to recall why her name was so familiar.

"Yes, Karis! We were in K-3 together at Evangel. And my Mother taught you and your sister piano. We used to have play dates all the time until we were eight."

"*O-M-G! Karis*! What in the world? I thought you all moved," I squealed as I hugged her. I remembered. It was coming back to me.

"Calm down girl before you get us in trouble!" she said, tugging my arms away from her neck. I quickly got myself together and looked around to make sure I hadn't made too much of a scene. Too late. Coach Blanding was already looking over in our direction.

"Karis, how have you been? When did you all move back into the area? Where do you live? Why didn't you say anything to me yesterday?" all my questions spilled out in one breath. I struggled to re-focus my attention to the task at hand.

"Girl, we can talk at lunch. Right now, we need to be focused on making this team," she said nudging me forward because I was next in line.

"Okay, Okay, Okay!" I said as I stepped onto the mat. I was so excited about seeing Karis I almost flipped right out of the gym.

After our first two sessions, Karis and I walked to lunch together catching up. I introduced her to the girls, and we spent the rest of the day talking between sessions. We talked so much that I was distracted from worrying about the impending cuts. By the time we were seated in front of the coaches waiting for first cuts at the end of the day, I felt way more relaxed than I imagined I would be.

As I watched the coaches walk to the front of the gym, I felt my stomach turn into knots. I took a deep breath and said a quick prayer. What's done is done and I've done my best. I can only pray that I made it.

Coach Courtney started talking and thanked us all for our hard work. She told us that those who made it to the next round were not going to be assigned to any specific team yet. We would simply be moving forward.

"I will call the numbers in numerical order. If you hear your number, Congratulations! We will see you in the morning. If you don't hear your number, please see Coach Newman for your evaluation," she explained, "We don't want you to walk away asking yourself why you didn't make the cut. We want you to understand what you need to work on so you can tryout again next season. So, without any further delay: *3, 12, 18...,*"

As she began calling out numbers, I scanned the room observing people as they realized that they hadn't made the team. Their faces clouded in disbelief and disappointment. A couple of the girls even began to cry.

"*.... 21, 23, 27...*" She continued almost in slow motion.

I closed my eyes as she came closer to my number and pleaded to God that she would not only call my number, but all of my friends' too.

"*39, 42, 43, 44......*" I squeezed Taylor's hand and tried not to squeal when I realized we had both made it to the second round. By the time Coach

Courtney had finished counting, I realized that all my friends had made it to the second round, even Karis. I tried to contain my excitement because I didn't want the girls who hadn't made it to feel bad because I was celebrating. But I couldn't help from grinning ear to ear.

"Congratulations, ladies. We will see you tomorrow morning at 9:00AM," Coach Courtney closed.

"Tomorrow! Tomorrow! We will see you tomorrow!" Taylor squealed as we jumped up and down hugging each other. "We are coming back tomorrow!" she shouted as Kennedy, Hayden and Zahla joined our happy dance circle.

"I am so relieved," said Hayden. "I don't think I have ever been so nervous in my life,"

"Me either," I admitted with a sigh of relief. "Now we just have to make the next cut,"

"Yeah. Yeah. I am just excited I made it through today," Kennedy chimed in. "These tryouts are hard. There are a lot of talented girls here,"

"I know right," Zahla agreed. "There were only about 15 girls cut today and there are only 50 spots, but there are still over 100 girls here," she pointed out.

"Well at least you all can count!" Someone interrupted as a group of girls walked by.

"What? I know y'all are *not* talking to us!" Kennedy snapped back without missing a beat.

Kennedy has never been the kind of person to let foolishness slide and I knew this time would not be any different. I quickly grabbed her by her arm and pulled her into the hall.

"G-u-r-r-l! You know you have to ignore ignorance. They're just trying to psych us out," I told her.

"They're trying to do what?" she frowned.

"Psych us out...You know. Try to get us to lose focus, to let them get under our skin," I explained.

"Well mission accomplished," she said rolling her head almost 360 degrees.

"Kennedy, we don't even know those girls, and I am pretty sure they are singling us out because they see how good we are. They probably feel a little threatened. Ignore them and remember we are not just being evaluated on our skills, but our behavior too," I reminded her just as the coaches came walking out of the gym.

"Okay Amira, but they better not try me again because I can't guarantee what I am going to do," she warned nudging me in the shoulder.

"I got your back Kennedy, and you know I am going to hold you down," I giggled. "I am going

to hold you down, so you won't beat anyone up,"
I laughed as I jumped onto her back.

Laughing we walked outside, to wait for our rides.
The rest of the girls followed closely behind re-
capping the events of the day. No one got too
worked up over Kennedy's reaction because
that's who she is and that's what she does. Since
we'd been little, Kennedy was always the
protector of the group. If you came after one of
us, you were coming after her too. We were more
than just friends at this point, we were like sisters.

CHAPTER 19

Why in the world is she here? I thought when my sister, Aukema, picked us up from practice. Aukema had just started her freshman year at Spelman with dual enrollment, at Georgia Tech, in some type of science and math program. Dual enrollment is just a fancy way to say she goes to two schools at the same time. I am not even sure how that works, but I know my parents didn't have to pay for any of it because she received a ridiculous amount of money in scholarships.

She really wanted to go to an HBCU, a Historically Black College and University, and she'd also really wanted to go to Georgia Tech, because it had one of the best Biotech Engineering programs in the country. Whatever that is. Plus, Dad had gone to graduate school there. It was like killing two birds with one stone.

I didn't really pay her too much attention because Taylor, Zahla, and I were too busy sharing highlights of the day. By the time we pulled into the driveway, I just had to ask.

"Why are you here? I thought you were supposed to be in school?" I questioned.

"Mommy and Daddy have to go check on Nana and she didn't want to leave you all home alone overnight. Plus, we are on break, so I decided to come home," she answered.

"Nana? What's wrong with Nana?" I asked as we were getting out of the car. Nana is my Grandmother's Mother. She is 100 years old.

"She's old Amira!" she said sarcastically.

"I know she's old Aukema! She's been old for years, but what's wrong with her? Why are

Mommy and Daddy going to check on her?" I snapped becoming agitated.

"I am sorry!" she apologized for being flippant. "She has been in and out of the hospital for the last couple of weeks, and they just wanted to get a better understanding of what's going on,"

Before the car came to a complete stop in the driveway, I jumped out leaving Taylor and Zahla behind without saying goodbye so I could go speak to my parents. When I got into the house their bags were already by the door.

"What happened? When are you leaving? How long will you be gone? How is Grandma Lil' Babe?" I blurted out not giving them an opportunity to answer any of the questions.

"Slow down Amira. She's fine. She is at home resting. However, we just wanted to go and check on her to make sure that everything is okay," Mom tried to assure me.

"So why are you leaving in the middle of the week? Why not wait until the weekend when we all can go?" I asked, not fully convinced by her answer.

"Because we can," Daddy answered. "Why should we wait until the weekend? Your mother and I have the luxury of being able to work from anywhere so we can pick up and leave whenever we want," I have always hated when my parents went out of town, especially when my Mom had to travel. I let it go because I knew if I said anything else Daddy would have gone on forever.

"We'll be back in a few days, and you know all you have to do is call or FaceTime us. You know I am going to miss you and I really wanted to be here for your entire tryouts, but we have to go check on Nana," Mom said.

"Okay Mommy, I understand. I just wish you could be here too, but I know Nana is more important. Plus, I am going to FaceTime you every day anyway," I warned her knowing there was really nothing I could do about the situation.

"So enough about leaving. Did you make the cut?" My mom asked shifting the conversation.

"I made it! I made it!" I said jumping up and down forgetting she was about to leave.

"Congratulations! I am so proud of you. So, what's the next steps?" she asked equally excited.

"To be honest mom I have no clue," I admitted.

"Huh? Why?" she inquired a bit confused.

"Well right after Coach Courtney read all our numbers, a group of girls walked by talking junk," I explained.

"What does that have to do with anything?" she said still a bit confused.

"Well Kennedy jumped up and was about to go in, so I had to grab her and take her into the hallway before the coaches noticed anything," I went on.

"Enough said," she chuckled. "I swear some things never change! Kennedy has been doing that since you all were little girls. Well I will be praying for your success. Give me some suga. Daddy and I have to get on the road," She kissed me as she walked out the door.

CHAPTER 20

Unlike my mother, my sister Aukema is always super early for everything. She had me up at the crack of dawn to get ready. By the time I made it downstairs, my little brother had already been, bathed, dressed, and fed. Aukema even had Freddie at the table eating, and he is always the last to rise.

"Good Morning everyone," I sang my greeting to my siblings. I guess I was in an especially good mood because I had made it through the first round of tryouts. I patted Aukema on the back, gave Ellis a big hug and a kiss, and smacked Freddie in the back of the head.

"Why are you up so early?" I asked Freddie.

"Why are you all in my business?" He responded not answering the question.

"Because your business is my business boy!" I said nudging him in the back of the head again.

"He wanted me to drop him off at the gym, so he could get his workout in," Aukema interjected not wanting to hear our customary banter. "So, I told him if he wanted to go, I wasn't making two trips. He needed to be dressed and ready to go when I left the house,"

"Wow! That's a first! His feet usually don't hit the floor until about noon," I teased.

"Well, Captain Aukema is here! And you know she will leave me without a second thought. I figured I wouldn't test her, especially since Mom isn't here to defend me," he joked.

"Ha, Ha," Aukema laughed. "Eat your food and get your skinny tail in the car," We knew Aukema wasn't really joking. "Amira, tell Taylor to meet us outside."

"Already done," I answered as I saluted her.

****

By the time I got outside, Taylor and Freddie were already chatting it up in the car.

"What do you think we are going to do today?" I interrupted.

"I am not sure," Taylor replied. "But Coach Courtney mentioned something about a small group session when you were dragging Kennedy into the hallway,"

"Oh, I wonder what that could be?" I responded talking aloud to myself as we pulled up in the front of the school.

Today, Aukema had us at the school so early, there was no need to rush. Taylor and I grabbed our things and went into one door and Freddie went into another. We arrived so early that we were literally the first ones there besides the coaches. And when we walked into the gym, it was so silent you could hear a pin drop.

Then Coach Blanding broke the silence. "Good Morning ladies. Come on in," she welcomed. "How are you doing this morning?"

"Fine," we answered in unison.

"Are you all excited about today?" Coach Newman asked.

"Yes." We did it again.

Coach Courtney started to laugh. "Hey, are you girls' sisters or something?" she teased.

"No," we answered again.

She laughed again. "Then why are you all answering in unison?" She asked. Taylor and I just stared at each other.

"It's okay girls don't be nervous," Coach Lewis said. "What are your names?"

"I am Amira, and this is Taylor," I answered.

"Have you all been cheering long?" Coach Lewis asked.

"Yes. About seven years," we responded in chorus again.

"Wow! Both of you?" Coach Newman exclaimed.

"Yes," We both responded again.

They all laughed as Taylor and I stared at each other in disbelief.

"Don't worry girls. It happens to the best of us," Coach Newman laughed. "Nerves make us do silly things. Just do your best and most importantly, have fun," she said as they walked towards the front of the gymnasium. After the coaches walked away Taylor and I just looked at each other.

"What was that?" She asked.

"I have no clue. I guess we're nervous and even a little shocked that they were even talking to us," I speculated.

"Maybe," she shrugged. "I hope that doesn't happen again, or else they are going to think that something is wrong with us,"

****

"*Hola!* Chicas," Coach Newman sang from the front of the gym.

"*Hola,* Coach Newman," we all sang back in unison.

"Today is going to be a bit different from the past two days. Today, you are going to spilt up into groups of between 10 and 15 girls. And we want you to choreograph a 5 to 8 minute half time routine. The routine should include all the elements we have been working on for the past two days. We are looking for proper technique, teamwork, and most importantly, creativity. You will have the entire day to work on your routine and you all will perform tomorrow before lunch. After lunch, we'll announce the teams for Freshmen, JV, and Varsity. So, choose wisely and let's get started," Coach Newman instructed.

As the gym filled with chatter Coach Blanding raised her hand to get everyone's attention. "Just remember ladies we are here to help so please do not hesitate to ask for assistance if you need it,"

After the coaches' announcements, we all huddled without hesitation to come up with a game plan, Kennedy, Zahla, Hayden, Taylor and me. First on the agenda we had to add some more girls to the group.

"What about her?" Zahla asked pointing to a girl with freckles who was standing across the room.

"What about her?" Kennedy probed.

"She was in my group and she can really tumble. She can also be lifted for stunts," Zahla responded ignoring Kennedy's disparaging response.

"Well if you think she can hang, go ask her if she wants to be a part of our group," Taylor said.

As Zahla ran across the gym to recruit the girl with the red hair, I quickly ran over to recruit Karis. Hayden and Taylor also found two other girls while Kennedy just stood there inspecting every girl from head to toe.

"Okay we need one more girl," I pointed out as I looked around the circle. "What about you Kennedy. You're the only one who hasn't recruited anyone. Have you noticed anyone who might be a good fit for the group?"

"I don't know," she said dismissively. "I am not sure if any of these girls can really hang with us.

You know we go hard," she hesitated as she rolled her eyes with her hands on her hips shifting her weight back and forth.

"Well you need to make a decision because we have all picked someone. We have to have at least 10 people in the group, but you're the only one who hasn't picked anyone," Hayden said trying to get her to pick someone.

"You tried it. Don't rush me Hayden. This is important. I don't want anyone messing up our opportunity to make the team," Kennedy said almost dismissing Hayden altogether as she scanned the gymnasium. "What about her?" She said pointing to an extra curvy, tall girl standing on the other side of the gym. "She was in my group and she could really hold her own,"

Well I know Kennedy had noticed her talent, but I was also wondering if it had registered how much the two of them looked alike? That girl could have been Kennedy's twin.

"Go ask her!" Taylor blurted out. "We don't have all day. We need to get started,"

****

Once we had solidified our team, Zahla ran over to the coaches to be clear on the instructions. She was there and back in what seemed to be two seconds flat.

"Creativity," she repeated. "They not only want us to be technically sound, they are looking for creativity and teamwork. And the rest is up to us,"

The instructions seemed simple enough. So, we started to develop our routine. We all agreed we should include, dance, cheer, tumbling, stunts, and step. We also agreed that because of time limitations, we would break up into five groups to choreograph each part and come back together to teach each other the parts.

"We need to be high energy and impact," I reminded the girls. "So, don't over- complicate things,"

We agreed that we would pair up with the person we recruited to arrange our part of the routine. Afterwards, we would all come back together to teach each other our parts before lunch and then practice our entire routine together after lunch.

The morning flew by and lunch came and went before we knew it. We had been working so hard to put the routine together, none of us had even noticed that the day was about to end when the coaches called us all back to the main gym.

"Welcome back ladies. We can see that you all have been working very hard, and we are excited about your presentations tomorrow. Go home and rest. We will see you bright and early tomorrow," Coach Courtney announced.

Rest? Rest? Who was going to rest? We all had already agreed that everyone was coming over to Taylor's and my house to practice. Taylor and Zahla had already called their Moms to come over to critique us and help us to tighten up our routine and Taylor had already texted her brother Tyler to create a music re-mix for our routine.

By the time Aukema, arrived we were all standing outside ready to go. Of all the days for her to be late, why'd she picked this one? To be honest, she wasn't late. The coaches had released us early. I had to wait for her for the first time in my life. She'd barely come to a complete stop before Taylor, Kennedy, Hayden, Zahla, and I piled into the truck.

"What in the world?" She hollered when we all started piling into the truck. "You better be glad I picked up Freddie early and he's home with Ellis, or else you all wouldn't be able to fit,"

"Sorry, I totally forgot to text you to tell you that everyone is coming over tonight to practice," I apologized.

"Well before you do anything else, make sure you FaceTime Mommy when you get home. She said she wants to talk to you," she said.

"Why? Is there something wrong? Is Nana okay?" I asked immediately concerned.

"No, nothing is wrong, and Nana is fine. She just asked me to tell you to call her when you got home," she assured me.

"Okay," I sighed in relief.

After talking to Mommy for a few minutes, I ran outside to join the girls hoping that I hadn't missed too much. When I walked outside Karis' mother Mrs. O was dropping her off.

"Hey Ms. O!" I shouted with excitement as I greeted her through the open window of the car.

"Hey Amira! The last time I saw you, you were a little girl. How are you doing? Is your Mom home?" She greeted me.

"No Ma'am. She and my Dad went out of town to check on my Nana," I informed her.

"Oh, I hope she's okay," she said with concern.

"She's fine, she's just getting old and my parents wanted to check on her," I assured her.

"Okay. Tell her I said hello, and I will reach out to her when she returns," she said as she was driving away.

"I will" I shouted as Karis and I ran to the back yard.

It was like old times again. Coach Dee and Dominique stood over us like hawks making sure the execution of our routine was seamless and flawless.

"Well I don't know why…," Coach Dee said nonchalantly in her southern twang as she rolled her neck with her hands on her hips, "… Y'all even asked us to come out here and look at this…"

My heart sank with every word.

"… Because y'all seem to have everything together. It looks great ladies and they would have to be blind and crazy not to select every single one of you," she said smiling as proud as a peacock.

"You all look fabulous," Coach Dominique chimed in. "It looks like we have done our jobs Dee," she bragged as they both turned and walked into the house closing the door behind them.

I was in absolute shock. It had never been that easy to please the two of them. It was always something: "'*Be louder! Work harder! Jump higher!* '" Their approval was such a surprise I thought I was going faint.

"Okay. Okay. So, let's quit while we are ahead and talk about our outfits, make-up, and the game plan for tomorrow" Kennedy said snapping us back into reality.

After a few minutes we were all on the same page about the outfit and the make-up, and we all agreed to arrive no later than 8:00AM to practice one more time before the presentations began.

When I walked into the house, I was exhausted and starving. I sat down to eat dinner, but my nerves wouldn't let me enjoy the food. So, I put it away in the refrigerator, to enjoy tomorrow. I went upstairs to take a shower and when I was finished getting my things ready for the next day, I fell asleep before my head could hit the pillow.

CHAPTER 21

This is it. Today is the day, the last day of tryouts. I got up extra early because I wanted to make sure I had everything we discussed for our routine. We all agreed to wear something with sparkle on the top, no matter the color and a coordinating bow, a high-top ponytail, and black shorts with white sneakers. That way we were coordinating without having to worry about being *"too matchy, matchy,"*

When I finished getting dressed, I texted Taylor to make sure Tyler had finished the mix for our routine. I wanted to make sure the timing was perfect. We didn't want to have to rely on someone hitting the stop and start button during our routine. The margin for error was just too great. She texted me back as I was going downstairs to eat. She said everything was perfect. She had even gone through the routine a few times to make sure.

I walked to the kitchen really missing my Mom. On a day like to today, she would have had a hot, hardy breakfast on the table waiting for me. I could just taste it, the crispy bacon, fluffy eggs, buttery grits, sweet honey biscuits, and the fluffy blueberry pancakes. I would have never eaten all that food before a day like today, but the gesture meant everything. All Aukema had to offer was a fruit and yogurt parfait. I guess it was better than nothing, considering she knew it was my favorite go to breakfast.

I took my time eating breakfast because I wanted to make sure I didn't get an upset stomach from eating too fast. I drank some pineapple juice and lots of water. I wanted to make sure I was properly hydrated for the day. I even caught a few Cheerios' in my mouth as Ellis threw them from his chair. As I was finishing breakfast, I could hear Taylor tapping on the storm door glass as she walked into the house. She was not really asking for permission to enter. It was more like an announcement of her arrival.

"I am in the kitchen," I shouted, letting her know my whereabouts.

"Okay, are you ready to go?" She hollered back.

"Yes! Let me grab my bag," I answered. "Do you have the music?"

"Yes! Don't be such a worry wart. I will let you listen to it in the car," she replied as she walked back out the door heading for the car.

"I just want to make sure it's right!" I yelled knowing she couldn't hear me as she walked out the door.

****

Taylor was right. The mix was perfect. Tyler had the timing right from the intro, to the dance combination, to the finale. She's right I am a worry wart, but I just want the routine to be perfect.

When we arrived at school, all the girls were waiting outside, even Hayden, and she's never on time. We all agreed that we would meet early to go through the routine a few more times with the music. But we weren't the only ones with that plan.

The girls who had been extra sassy to Taylor, for no reason, earlier in the week were there too, and by the look on Kennedy's face she was ready to take care of some unfinished business. As we made our way to the door, there were hard stares from both sides. I was just praying they wouldn't give Kennedy any excuse to say something, but before I could finish my prayer, the same girl just had to say something.

"Oh, the freshmen are here early to practice their routine… as if that is going to make a difference," she remarked in a tone as if she were talking to a baby.

"I bet we'll be good enough to take your spot," Kennedy fired back.

"Yeah, right. I would love to see that happen," the girl taunted.

"Well make sure you get a front row seat, because you're not going to want to miss this," Kennedy said as she mocked the girl's arrogance moving way too close to her for my comfort.

"Okay, we'll see," Karis interrupted as she stepped between the two girls grabbing Kennedy and walking away. "Stop talking all that trash and let your performance speak for itself,"

"Don't worry, we are going to bring it," the girl yelled after us.

"Really! *Bring it*? She sounds like an old tired movie. Come on y'all. Let's stay focused. We don't have time for this. We have to practice our routine," Taylor insisted as we walked into the gymnasium.

What's wrong with that girl? Why is she all up in our space? I said to myself. I felt my phone vibrating in my bag and wondered who was calling as I searched for my phone.

"Mommy, Mommy!" I squealed as I answered the video call.

"Good Morning Amira!" She giggled in response to my excitement. "I know you are at the last day of tryouts, but I wanted to let you know that I am praying for your success and I know you will do your best,"

"Thank you, Mommy. I really wish you were here," I responded, a bit distracted by the morning's drama.

"Why baby? What's going on?" she pressed.

"Well...," I said as I began to explain the whole ordeal with that girl over the past few days.

"Well honey...," she began. "Sometimes that's how people act when they feel jealous or threatened. Just do what you do best and let the coaches do the rest,"

"Thank you, Mommy. I really needed that. I love you, but I have to go," I said as I blew her kisses rushing her off the phone.

No sooner than I had put my phone away, the coaches came to the front of the gymnasium to get the day started. There were no long speeches or even small talk. They just gave each squad a number and told us that we would be performing in that order. We were number 7 out of 9 groups, and there was no extra time to practice. We just had to sit, watch, and wait.

The routines lasted about 3 to 5 minutes and I began to get a little worried because our routine was 7 minutes 56 seconds to be exact. I hope it wasn't going to be too much, but it's what we choreographed and there was no time to change it.

As the first group started to perform, I could feel my stomach churning into knots. I knew I'd better get up and go to the bathroom before it was too late. I didn't want my nerves to get the better of me so I would end up either peeing on myself *or* throwing up in the middle of our routine. I have seen girls do both, and I didn't want either of those scenarios! So as soon the first group finished, I jumped up and race walked to the bathroom.

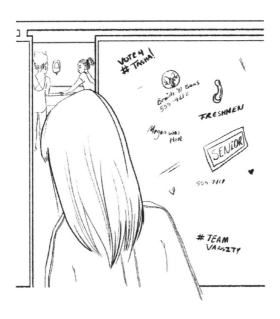

The bathroom was pretty much empty, but I could hear that there was someone else in one of the stalls taking care of her business and I wasted no time handling mine. When I finished and came out to wash my hands, she was standing at the sink washing her hands. Yep, that same girl who had been giving us a hard time all week.

"Oh! Hello," I spoke, not knowing what else to do or say.

"Hey," she responded shortly as if she couldn't be bothered to say much more.

"My name is Amira," I continued, not wanting to be rude in an already extremely awkward moment.

"And?" she snarled. "Why would that be important to me?"

Taken a little aback, I responded the only way I knew how. "Well I thought you just might want to know the name of one of the people you have been trying to bully and intimidate this week,"

"Well now we can see why you don't get paid for thinking," She tried to insult me without giving me a second look.

Now I had a choice to make. I could snap back at her for that tired dis or I could take the high road and just walk away. "All the same, I wish you be best," I said, deciding to take the high road as I finished washing my hands and she walked out the bathroom.

I stood there staring at my reflection in the mirror trying to calm my nerves and collect myself when I heard another bathroom stall door open. I didn't even realize there was someone else there.

"Don't take offense Amira, Karla has been doing that to people for years. She's nothing but an insecure bully, but no one has ever challenged her or reported her," Coach Newman said as she came out of the stall. "But she has certainly met her match with your little crew,"

I gave her a nervous giggle in complete and utter shock that she even knew my name, and secondly, that there was someone else in the bathroom, not to mention a coach.

"No worries. It's like First Lady Michelle Obama said, "'*When they go low, we go high,*'" she continued as she washed her hands looking at my reflection in the mirror. I still couldn't find the words to respond. I just looked at her trying to force myself to respond.

"It's okay, Chica. You did the right thing," she said as she patted my shoulder and walked towards the door.

"Thank you," I finally uttered so she wouldn't think I was a complete dunce.

"What took you so long? They are already on group number five," Taylor chastised me as soon as I sat down.

"I can't even begin to tell you, but the girl that keeps harassing us, her name is Karla," I said, dropping her a nugget to satisfy her curiosity until I could tell her the whole story.

"What? What happened?" She pressed as she grabbed my arms looking me directly into my eyes.

"Shhhhhh, you are making a scene," I whispered. "I'll tell you later," I promised hoping to appease her. "We are up next, and we have to go get in place," I said changing the subject as I motioned to the other girls to get up and huddle for a quick prayer and waited for our number.

"Group number seven," called Coach Lewis.

"Okay. This is it. We have to go hard, or we are going home," said Kennedy in her attempt to give us a pep talk. "So, let's do this!"

The music started and there was no turning back. We strutted, we danced, we cheered, we stepped, we jumped, we stunted, and we flipped. There wasn't an element we didn't cover in our routine and for the finale, we tossed Zahla and Hayden so far into the air they could have touched the rafters. When we finished, there was nothing, no applause, no cheers. It was dead silent. We just stood there staring at one another panting trying to figure out what went wrong and who messed up because after all the other groups there was at least a respectable amount of applause to acknowledge their efforts.

Then all at once the gym erupted, and in that moment I could breathe again. We delivered, and everyone was on their feet. Well everyone except Karla and her crew. Even the coaches were smiling and clapping. I am not sure what we did, but it was obviously good enough to get everyone's attention, and hopefully it was good enough for everyone to make one of the squads. Now all we could do is wait.

All the squads finished right before lunch as scheduled. When the Coaches stood, I was on pins and needles. I grabbed Taylor's hand, she grabbed Zahla's, and Zahla grabbed Hayden's. Without a second thought, our whole team sat hand in hand with anticipation.

As Coach Courtney stepped forward with a piece of paper in her hand, she began by saying.

Making The Squad

"Ladies you have made it extremely difficult for us this year. The level of talent and enthusiasm has been the best we have seen in years. This year we are going to do something we have never done before, and we are so excited about the direction of our teams. Instead of waiting until after lunch to announce the teams, we are going to do it now. We are going to announce the Freshman team first, then the Junior Varsity team and lastly the Varsity team. If you didn't make a team, we encourage you to try again next season. So, without any further delay, on our Freshman squad this year: Doralis, Sharonda, Kara, Shona, Erica, Amy, Julie..."

She read off at least 15 names, but she didn't call any of ours. My heart sank and I could feel the tears welling up in my eyes, but I didn't dare let a tear fall. I tried to stay optimistic. Maybe we made the Junior Varsity squad. How cool would that be?

"…Now for our Junior Varsity squad, Lori Joe, Erica T, Jackie, Paula…," the Coach read more names off the list.

Wait! Those are the girls we recruited to be in our group. Taylor and I squeezed each other's hand in anticipation.

"…Karla…," she continued.

Karla! What? How did she make the team? I was screaming in agony on the inside.

"...Kim, Katina..." She must have read at least five or six more names. "Okay now for the Varsity Squad..."

I was completely floored. None of us had made the team? I just cupped my face with my hands and waited for her to finish reading the names so this nightmare could be over.

"Vanessa, Senovia, Tene, Ty, Denise F, Denise A, ..."

I couldn't hold back my tears any longer, and it was as if someone had opened the flood gates of heaven. I just hung my head down and hoped no one could hear me.

"Carol, Kennedy, Hayden...," she continued.

Did she just say Hayden and Kennedy! Kennedy and Hayden made the squad? My tears began to slow down.

"Zahla, Karis, Tammy, ..."

Well at least my girls made the squad and I was happy about that. But, what had I done wrong? What had Taylor done wrong? It was probably that whole run-in with Karla. But she'd made a team.

"...Taylor, Kitra...," She continued.

Taylor? Did she say Taylor? My heart skipped a beat.

"And last, but certainly not least, Amira," she concluded.

Making The Squad

When I heard my name, I was sure I had jumped out of my skin, hit my head on the rafters and fainted from the impact. When I opened my eyes all the girls were piled on top of me screaming and hollering.

We did it! Not only did we make the squad, we made Varsity.

When all the excitement had died down, Coach Courtney gave us the practice details and told us that she would see us on Monday. When she was finished, I bolted across the gymnasium to call Mom. I must have called her at least five or six times with no answer. I was so disappointed because I couldn't wait to tell her what had happened.

We gathered our things and went outside to wait for Aukema to pick us up, but when we got outside all our parents were waiting with flowers and balloons.

I ran towards my Mother almost knocking her down.

"We made it! We made it!" I squealed with excitement.

"I know, I know," she laughed with joy.

"How did you know?" I paused.

"After seeing your routine, Coach Dee and Coach Dominque said that the coaches would be blind not to put you on the team. So, Daddy and I rushed home to make sure we could be here to celebrate your big day."

"Mommy we didn't make the Freshman team," I told her.

"What?" she asked, a bit confused. "I thought you said you made the squad?"

"We did Mommy! We made Varsity!" I shouted.

"What! Varsity?" She shouted back, "Well I guess the Fab 5 strikes again,"

"Yep, Mommy. The Fab 5 strikes again!" I proclaimed.

ABOUT THE AUTHOR

Tasha Fuller is the author of many popular picture books including *It's Bath Time Baby. Little Freddie's In A Zone. Mommy, I Want to be a Princess. and Mommy, I Want to Dance.* Tasha writes about her children, and *Making the Squad* is no different. She has taken the experiences of her daughters Amira and Aukema, along with her own, to create a wonderful story that all readers can relate. Tasha is a self-published author and publishing coach.